Friends and Lovers

Ellen Boneparth

authorHOUSE

AuthorHouse™
1663 Liberty Drive
Bloomington, IN 47403
www.authorhouse.com
Phone: 833-262-8899

© 2020 Ellen Boneparth. All rights reserved.

No part of this book may be reproduced, stored in a retrieval system, or transmitted by any means without the written permission of the author.

Published by AuthorHouse 10/09/2020

ISBN: 978-1-6655-0355-6 (sc)
ISBN: 978-1-6655-0354-9 (e)

Print information available on the last page.

Any people depicted in stock imagery provided by Getty Images are models, and such images are being used for illustrative purposes only.
Certain stock imagery © Getty Images.

This book is printed on acid-free paper.

Because of the dynamic nature of the Internet, any web addresses or links contained in this book may have changed since publication and may no longer be valid. The views expressed in this work are solely those of the author and do not necessarily reflect the views of the publisher, and the publisher hereby disclaims any responsibility for them.

~ *2012* ~

"Hi."

Jen recognized Mark's voice immediately. Grinning, she said, "Hello to you. Has it been a year?"

"More, I think. How are you?"

She took a deep breath. "The world has gone to hell, except for Obama, but personally, I'm doing fine. Where are you?"

"Walking in the hills behind Stanford."

"Lucky you. I'm in my cramped office near Capitol Hill."

He laughed. "Listen, sometimes reception cuts out in these hills. Can I call back if we lose each other?"

Running a finger though her graying hair, she said, "We lose each other often, don't we? And one of us eventually calls back."

"Yeah, that kind of happens."

She pictured his tanned face, lean build, sandy hair. "It's been happening for a lot of years."

"Seventeen."

"Wow. That long. You're one of my oldest friends."

"You, too. Can you talk?"

"I've gotta meet Nathan in twenty minutes. I've got about ten."

"Good." He paused. "You're not in Africa."

"I've been going less often," Jen replied. "Too long a trip. I've got a young assistant who goes over to vet our grantees."

"Got it. I'm thinking of giving up marathons."

"Hey, you're the younger one. Four years, as I recall."

"Four years on two hopeless knees."

"So, we're decrepit old friends." Jen could see him smiling, green eyes twinkling.

"That won't change. You know, I…"

The line went dead. She glared at her cell, shook it as if that would help. She called back. No connection. She lay the phone down on her desk, gathered the papers she needed to take home, stuffed them in her canvas shoulder bag. She stared at her phone, willed it to ring, checked her watch.

No time now. Nathan would be waiting at the Library of Congress. She stuffed her phone in the pocket of her trench coat and flew out of the office.

~ 1995 ~

Chapter 1

Jennifer Jacobs, one of Hunter College's most popular professors, would never have considered university administration before she was contacted by Macaulay Honors College in the CUNY system. A tenured professor of history, she had a full life – teaching, researching social history, living in and exploring Manhattan's Greenwich Village. She would, perhaps, have enjoyed a more fulfilling relationship with the man in her life, Dan Levine, but they both devoted themselves to their careers and their freedom to do so made things work.

Macaulay Honors College, however, was something different from the eleven other colleges in the City University of New York. The small campus, serving only a couple of hundred students, occupied a mid-rise building on West 67th Street. It offered courses, interdisciplinary seminars linked to aspects of New York City life, that expanded on the student's normal curriculum. Its students, drawn from the top four percent of the city's high school graduates, were a diverse lot who had earned their honors privileges with outstanding performances in high school. Their privileges included free tuition over four years, a laptop computer, and a heavy dose of academic and career counseling.

Jen had met many Macauley honors students, usually the exceptional performers in her classes at Hunter. Whenever, over the years, she'd been invited to participate in a seminar at Macauley, she'd jumped at the opportunity to teach the city's brightest and cooperate with creative faculty from other CUNY colleges and disciplines.

When asked to be a candidate for the job of dean at Macauley, Jen quickly accepted. While the dean's job brought with it the bureaucratic hassles of college administration, it also meant developing exciting new curricula, trying out innovative pedagogy, and grooming students already on a leadership track. The interview process involved two days of immersion in seminars, faculty meetings, and interviews with Macauley's trustees. She sensed her candidacy was well received.

Jen's selection as Dean was announced two days after her interview. To celebrate, Dan, her lawyer friend, invited her to dinner, one of the rare occasions he broke free early from work. She dressed for the occasion in a black wool pantsuit and a deep pink silk blouse.

On a crisp Fall evening, he met her at a tiny French bistro near Macaulay with a gift in hand. Once they were seated, he presented it along with a short toast. "For the desk of a dean who will doubtless put Macauley on the map."

"Don't say that too loud," she murmured. "Many think it's already on the map."

He shrugged. "Never heard of it 'til I met you."

Refraining from a retort, Jen slid her finger through the silver paper. Inside was a burgundy desk calendar, the aroma of new leather tickling her nose. Her initials were monogrammed in gold, the kind of accessory more appropriate to a corporate suite than a crammed college office with an ugly metal desk. Nonetheless, she thanked Dan warmly. He was a generous person who loved giving gifts.

"This weekend is full of treats," she continued cheerfully. "First, this dinner and tomorrow an overnight in the Berkshires."

He brushed back salt and pepper hair off his forehead. "Actually, I can't do the Berkshires. I've got a public offering next week. I've got to be in the office all day tomorrow proofreading documents."

She bit her lip. "Do you realize how many times you've cancelled our plans because of work?"

"Listen, the only reason I'm here tonight is because I'm working tomorrow. Why don't you go with one of your friends? You can take my car."

"That's not the point. I wanted to spend time with you."

"Sorry. The firm comes first."

It always did, she thought, but said no more to avoid squabbling over dinner.

∼

When Jen got back to her Greenwich Village apartment, she took in the view of tenth street from the fifth floor. It was a busy Friday night, lines of honking cars maneuvering along the street toward Broadway. It would be so lovely to escape for the weekend.

She called her close friend and colleague Isabelle from Hunter's French Department. "Want to see the fall colors in the Berkshires tomorrow?"

"Much as I'd love to, I can't. I thought you were going with Dan."

She wound a finger through her chestnut hair. "He cancelled. Work."

"Jennifer, the two of you work hard and leave each other room for that. Okay. But what do you get out of the relationship?"

"Sometimes I wonder. He's smart, loyal, generous—"

"And rarely around. You can do better."

"There haven't been many white knights galloping up to my door."

"Open the door and see what happens."

They chatted about Jen's new job, noting happily they'd both still be working in Manhattan's sixties, only on different sides of Central Park. That made it easy to meet for lunch or dinner, or amble through the park.

"What does your first week look like?" Isabelle asked.

"Well, in addition to getting acclimated, I've got to set up the first meeting of the General Education Task Force."

"Why you?"

"Everyone likes to come to West 67th Street and Macaulay has a lovely conference room on our top floor. And we don't offer general education courses, so everyone thinks I'll be neutral."

"Ha!"

"I agree. I think the idea of having a system-wide g.e. course is nuts. You can't offer the same course at all our campuses. They're so different."

"Glad I'm not in your shoes."

"How about dinner next Friday? I'll tell you all about it."

"Can't wait."

Chapter 2

The conference room, taking up all of Macauley's eighth floor, was spacious, with tall windows front and back, and, pulled back, light blue velveteen drapes that softened the view of the surrounding buildings. A square teak conference table surrounded by chairs took up the center of the room. Attractive but formal. Jen decided to put a vase of yellow and orange marigolds on each side of the table to brighten things up. From a nearby bakery, she ordered chocolate chip cookies for the coffee break.

Each of the system's twelve campuses had a faculty representative on the task force. As task force members took their seats, Jen was struck by the way they placed themselves. The three powerhouse campuses, by virtue of size, academic reputation, and faculty achievements – Brooklyn College, CCNY and Hunter – took center seats on each side of the table. Jen, as convenor, sat alone on the fourth side.

Immediately, the task force members, almost equally men and women, took up unit load, rapidly agreeing to maintain the current system with students taking one three-unit g.e. course in each their first two years. They also agreed g.e. courses should continue to be interdisciplinary and faculty should volunteer to teach them. The John Jay task force member asked what would happen if there weren't enough volunteers. A tricky subject, Jen deferred it until a later meeting.

Encouraged by the degree of harmony, she signaled the student servers, Allison and LaTisha, to bring in coffee and cookies for the break. Over coffee, everyone milled around, exchanging gossip. When Jen called the meeting back to order, the professors, checking their watches, quickly seated themselves, eager to finish the discussion and hop on subways home.

∽

Unfortunately, the next week, the second session on course content was far less harmonious. Every task force member had his or her own view on what should be covered and didn't hesitate to say so. Not just say so. Faculty members began shouting, waving notes in the air, hurling insults.

Jen broke into the whirling maelstrom of opinions. "Obviously, this is a contentious topic. We need a format for discussing content. I'll present one next week. For now, let's adjourn." She rose and pushed back her chair. "Everyone, have a good weekend."

∽

That evening, when she began reciting her woes to Isabelle on the phone, Isabelle broke in, proposing dinner the next evening at a Thai restaurant on Broadway. They met at 7 p.m. and sat at a table surrounded by large posters of Thai palaces, ruins, and, of course, the king. The room was soothing with low pink lights and young servers gliding quietly between the tables and kitchen.

Jen immediately ordered a carafe of wine. "I need this," she groaned. "The meeting was a debacle."

Isabelle tied back her abundant black curls. "I'm surprised you're surprised. Faculty have deeply vested interests in g.e."

"Why?"

"Some want to star in the courses and lure freshmen to their majors. Others don't want to waste time teaching introductory material when they could be offering specialized upper division courses. A few don't want to teach at all."

The waiter brought their curry and noodle dishes, and Jen grabbed her chopsticks. "Then it has nothing to do with content? In my department we thoroughly analyze content."

"That's a history department for you. For most faculty, a small number care about content; the rest have hidden agendas." Isabelle reached for a wonton with her fork. "You need pressure from outside. Find an expert to whip them into shape."

Jen frowned. "Like who?"

"Someone like Mark Anderson over at the CUNY Graduate Center."

"Anderson? The guy who just won the American Book Award for Nonfiction? He's head and shoulders above this crowd."

Isabelle slurped up some noodles. "That's why they might listen to him."

"Honey, I'm a big fan of Mark Anderson's work. I've read all his books. He's a superstar. He'd never do this."

"The worst he can say is 'no.' He might consider it a challenge." Isabelle picked up the carafe. "Another glass?"

"Most definitely."

∽

At her desk the next morning, Jen pushed aside the stack of memos in front of her and pondered Isabelle's suggestion. Certainly, the task force would behave better in front of an eminent scholar like Mark Anderson, but he'd never agree to help. And she felt too hesitant to ask.

She went back to her memos, but the task force kept popping into her mind. The thought of a repeat session like the last one was dreadful, but she had few options. As Isabelle had said, the worst Anderson could say was no. She slid over her laptop and began drafting an email, wondering how much to say about the second task force meeting. Maybe a phone call would be better. She could tailor her request to his initial reaction.

She pulled up the system's faculty directory on her computer and found his number and office hours. There was also a photo – high forehead, sandy hair combed back, thin face and lips, penetrating eyes, a hint of a smile. She knew his face from his book jackets. Brains and looks, an unbeatable combination.

She rested her head against the back of her chair and tried to work through a phone conversation. Nothing came. She looked again at his faculty entry. Office hours on Monday. He'd probably be in. She sat up straight, told herself to behave like a dean, not a wimp. It was only a request.

She picked up her phone. "Is this Professor Anderson?"

"It is. Who's calling?"

She took a deep breath. "Jennifer Jacobs from Hunter College."

"Ah, the new dean at Macaulay. Congratulations."

She was taken aback. "Thank you. I didn't expect you'd—"

"I love Macaulay, always follow what's happening. I even know about your g.e. task force."

She rolled her eyes. "Then you know, uh, that it—"

"Didn't go well."

"Yes. Professor Anderson, I won—"

"Call me Mark. You wonder where to go next."

"Honestly, I have no idea where to go next. I don't want a repeat performance."

There was a long pause then he said, "I have an idea but it may not be what you're looking for."

"Hey, I'm open to anything."

"Okay. I don't think you'll ever get wide agreement on specific content. The topic is too loaded."

"So it seems."

"But you could probably get agreement on a number of course themes. Then you could leave it up to each college to make up its own courses as long as they all treat the same themes."

Jen drew a large star on a piece of paper on her desk. "Professor Anderson—"

"Mark."

"Mark. I hear an intellectual historian at work, and, you know, it sounds just right. If the task force can do that, we could probably get the system's Academic Senate on board."

Now the plunge, asking him to help.

"If it would be useful," he continued, "I could lead the discussion as a resident intellectual historian."

Whoosh. What a relief. "Useful? It would be..." She didn't want to sound too needy. "We meet Thursdays at 3 p.m. at Macaulay, but if you can't come then, I can change—"

"I'll see you Thursday, Jennifer."

From somewhere, she found the nerve to say, "Jen."

"Fine. Mark and Jen."

"Thank you."

She hung up, put her hands to her cheeks, which she knew had turned pink from anxiety. Mark and Jen. He'd made it so simple, as if they were a team. Well, that worked.

She dashed off an email to the task force, enthusiastically announcing Thursday's visitor.

Chapter 3

Thursday morning, before the task force meeting, Jen asked her student assistant to bring several small orchid plants from her office to the conference room for decoration. She ordered brownies for the break — anything to lift the mood.

Mark Anderson showed up at her office fifteen minutes early, gave her hand a vigorous shake. He was even more attractive in person, she thought, as she offered him the chair in front of her desk. She was glad she'd worn a beige, brushed velveteen pantsuit and had let her wavy chestnut hair loose around her collar.

He began by saying, "Your journal articles are mostly about family and public policy. Right?"

She felt flattered he'd researched her. "Lately, I'm focusing mostly on women, particularly single women in the U.S."

"A big topic. Autobiographical?" he said, grinning.

"I guess. I'm single and forty-two, confronting the biological clock. At some point, it was motherhood or tenure and promotion. I chose the latter."

She wondered why she was telling him all that. He had a way of drawing her out.

"My wife's in her late thirties. She's got the same dilemma, even though she has a spouse who can help with child-rearing."

"Oh, she's an academic?"

"Close. A law student. She's in her second year at Columbia. She's put off motherhood for at least another year."

"Well, if you end up a child-minder, it'll be hard to churn out a book a year."

"Yup, that's my problem." He smiled. "Now tell me about the task force. Are the natives still restless?"

"I hope not. I bought brownies to keep them docile."

"Chocolate is good."

"We'll see. Shall we go up to the conference room?"

The buzzing in the conference room hushed the moment Mark and Jen walked in. They sat together at Jen's side of the conference table and she introduced him to a round of applause. She asked the task force members to introduce themselves by name, college, and discipline.

When they finished, Mark said, "You're a fine representation of our system, an excellent group for this job. How many of you have taught g.e. courses?"

Almost all raised their hands.

He left his seat, stood behind the table, his hands on the back of his chair. "This may surprise you but we're not going to discuss course content today. I don't believe any two courses could meet all of your preferences."

Many task force members broke into smiles.

"Instead," he continued, "we're going to talk about themes." He turned to Jen. "Dean Jacobs, may I write on the board?" He moved to the whiteboard behind him, grabbed a marker. "Okay. Let's see if we can list themes we'd like our students to examine in their first two years of college."

Hands immediately shot up. In the next few minutes, the faculty proposed a number of themes – equality, participation, culture, diversity, and so on. When the list had reached fifteen, Mark suggested a break. Jen waved at the student servers to bring in the coffee and brownies. During the break there were lively exchanges, with Mark circulating among the task force members. After fifteen minutes, he signaled to Jen, and she called everyone back to their seats.

Mark, returning to his place behind Jen's table, crossed his arms over his chest. "What do you suppose comes next?" he asked the group.

A man from Baruch College called out, "We choose the key themes."

Others nodded in agreement.

"I'd have to say 'yes and no.' Yes, choices have to be made. We can't cover fifteen themes in two courses. But who makes the choice?"

Furrowed brows, shrugs, no verbal responses. Finally, Jen spoke up. "As I understand it, that's the job of the task force."

"Yes, that would be a traditional way of doing things."

Her colleague from Hunter called out, "What's an untraditional way?"

Mark studied the faces around the room. "Why not ask the whole faculty to vote on the three most relevant themes? After all, they're the ones designing and teaching these courses."

Lots of nods and thumbs-up.

"And," Mark paused for a long moment, "why not also have the students vote? They're the ones obliged to take the courses."

That was unexpected. Everyone started talking at once, either supporting or rejecting Mark's proposal. Jen thought it was brilliant. Even if only a few students bothered to vote, it was a buy-in from students and a highly novel and democratic way to proceed.

At that point, Mark announced he would leave the task force to its work. He leaned over to whisper in her ear, "Your baby. Let me know what happens."

He headed to the door amidst loud chatter.

Jen rose and called for order, which took a couple of minutes. When she could be heard over the group, she said, "This proposal is as much a surprise to me as it is to you. It obviously needs more thought. It's almost five. Shall we take it up next week?"

The faculty members reached for their notes and briefcases.

"One minute," she called out. "This is a unique proposal. We need to analyze the pros and cons before we take it public. Can you can keep this confidential?"

A woman from CCNY said, "We've gotta keep our mouths shut. We need a plan before everyone starts to trash us."

She was cheered by the others.

While Jen was dubious the proposal would remain confidential, at least she'd be able to run it by the central administration before it saw the light of day. "Okay, everyone, try to keep this under wraps. The less said, the less pressure we'll be under." She cleared her throat. "Talk to each other if you must, but not anyone else. See you next Thursday."

The group left in unexpectedly subdued fashion. Confidentiality just might work.

∼

All Friday morning, Jen considered how to follow up with Mark. She liked his idea but wasn't sure the task force would rally behind it, even less so, the system administration. How to sell it? Had Mark thought that through? While she doubted he'd be in his office on a Friday, she could leave a message.

He called back at the end of the day and suggested they meet on Monday after his office hours. "I come uptown to get home. We could have a drink somewhere near your office and talk."

Jen was game. "There's a wine bar, Beaujolais, a couple of blocks away."

"I know it. I'll meet you there at 5:30."

"Great. Have a good weekend."

∼

Jen kept herself busy Saturday and Sunday, in part to distract herself from Monday's appointment, which made her both excited and anxious. She visited the Met with Olivia, a friend from her department, caught a documentary on immigration at NYU, cooked a pasta dinner at home for Dan on Saturday. Yet, even with a full schedule, her mind kept returning to Mark's g.e. proposal and, to be honest, to Mark himself.

She had a lot of questions for him that had nothing to do with general education. She was curious how he came up with the topics he wrote about. She also wondered how he spent his time when not cogitating. All academics needed time away from mental activities. Her most creative ideas came from her subconscious when she was relaxing or pursuing something extracurricular. She'd decided to research foreign nannies after watching the immigration film. How did it work for Mark? She'd like to know.

Put simply, she'd like to know him better.

Chapter 4

Typical end-of-October weather, Monday afternoon was cool and gray. Mark called out to Jen from the end of the block just before she stepped into Beaujolais.

"Nice way to end a dreary day," he said, catching up and holding the door.

She grinned. "We're here for happy hour – two for one – if you've got the time."

"I can make the time."

They sat at a table by the tinted window and ordered four small glasses of different reds to sample and some cheese sticks to munch on.

"That was quite an assignment you gave my task force," she began. "At first, I thought it would go smoothly, then you threw in student voting. Utter chaos."

"That sounds a bit extreme. I know some innovative schools where students play a big role on curriculum committees."

"I bet those are small, experimental colleges that cater to the counterculture."

"Most are, but it works."

"Well, CUNY is a lot more complex than Bard or Evergreen. I've been trying to figure out ways to involve our students that won't threaten faculty or administration."

The young, bubbly waitress delivered the wine with labels written on the coasters.

"That's a clever way to help us distinguish the grapes," Jen said.

They each began with a Bordeaux from the Rhone valley. Mark took a sip and smiled. "You'll like this one."

He reached into his pocket, pulled out a sheet of notebook paper and passed it to her. He had sketched out a process in which faculty in g.e. classes brought up the general idea of themes, asked students which ones interested them most, gave out ballots with the task force themes, and asked them to vote. Students not in g.e. classes could learn about the voting in their student newspapers which would have ballots in them.

"Well, I bet we'll get a good sample from the g.e. students," Jen said, "but I doubt many others will bother to vote."

"True, but you'd have a good response from the students most engaged in g.e. right now."

"Not a bad way to go. I'll try it out on the task force on Thursday."

"Let them exhaust their own ideas first. They might come up with something better. And please don't call it *my* idea. I'd like to fade from the scene completely."

"Leaving it on my plate."

He laughed. "Where it started. Want to about something other than g.e.?"

She nodded, reached for a cheese stick.

"What do you do for fun?"

"Well, I love to travel, but my friend Dan is pretty consumed with work. I do New York things – movies, museums, theater – and I work out at a gym, but that's necessity, not fun."

"You need to find exercise you enjoy. I burn lots of calories playing squash."

"Where do you play?"

"The Yale Club across from Grand Central."

"Oh yes, Yale. One of those small, experimental colleges you raved about," she teased.

"Well, I should have gone to one of them. The best thing Yale ever gave me was the Yale Club."

They chuckled.

"You said you play squash on the way home," she said. "Where's home?"

"Riverside Drive in the nineties. You?"

"The Village, near Washington Square Park, where, I know, I could jog, but jogging's worse than working out. Why do all the men I know push jogging?"

His eyebrows went up. "Even Dan?"

"No, not Dan." She laughed. "Maybe that's why we're together."

He was so easy to talk to. Despite all his credentials, he was completely down to earth. She felt like she'd known him a long time.

"You mentioned travel," Mark said. "Do you ever go to the New England History Association Conference? I don't think I've seen you there."

"You go? To such a plebeian group? I can't believe you get much intellectual stimulation there."

"You'd be surprised. A very interesting group and you also get to see beautiful parts of New England. It's at Bennington College this year, in three weeks. A chance to explore southern Vermont."

"The leaves will have fallen."

"Oh, some will be left. I can even give you a ride."

"That's kind. Let me think about it. I know the association has a strong women's caucus."

"There you go. Intellectual stimulation."

The waitress came by with the check, which Mark grabbed. Jen didn't fight him, simply saying she'd get the next one.

It was drizzling as they stepped outside and dashed for the subway.

"Let me know how the task force goes," he said. "And let me know about Bennington."

"I just might join you."

He smiled widely. "I'd like the company."

So would she.

~

On a local train with a number of stops until 4th Street, Jen mulled over her time with Mark Anderson. She had to admit she was attracted to him, even though that went against two of her rules. First, she never mixed work and play. It just got too complicated. She also avoided married men. She'd learned that lesson in her twenties.

Nonetheless, she thoroughly enjoyed his company. He brought spice to her life. And he really listened. He, a brilliant scholar, seemed interested in her, not just being polite. They had much more to talk about if only there were time and space.

So, was there anything wrong with colleagues going to a conference together? They'd have much more time to connect, and that weas something she really wanted.

~

On Thursday, the task force members had before them the matter of voting on g.e. themes. Jen sensed there was wide approval for a faculty vote. When she asked for a show of hands, it was unanimous.

She moved on. "Okay. Student voting. Your thoughts?"

Objections came from every direction.

"I've been thinking about this and I have an idea. First, it won't be hard to survey current g.e. students. Use a half hour of class time to get g.e. students to think about possible themes. Then, ask them to vote on the task force's list."

Most of the others endorsed that approach.

"And the rest? The non-g.e. students?" a professor from Staten Island called out.

"I admit that's harder," Jen responded, "but at least some students read their college newspaper. What if we took one section of the weekly paper to present our themes? We could have a ballot inserted in the paper."

Since it was close to five p.m., several task force members called for a vote. Jen put out two options: no appeal to non-g.e. students or an appeal in student newspapers. The newspaper appeal won. She thanked the task force members in glowing terms for their efforts. They thanked her for doing a good job as chair.

"No more cookies?" asked the representative from Queens College.

She chuckled. "Only if we have to return to the drawing board."

～

Friday morning Jen called Mark to let him know she'd borrowed his plan and it had been accepted.

"Clever woman. I knew you'd pull it off, even without brownies."

She basked in his compliment.

He cleared his throat. "What about Bennington? Are you coming?"

She'd decided to go. It was an opportunity to be with him which wasn't likely to happen in everyday life. "I'd like to come and would welcome a ride. I checked with the association, and they still have some free rooms in the dorm."

"Dorm? Listen, I'm staying in a colonial house near campus. Big fireplace. Three bedrooms. You can stay with me rent-free."

She felt her cheeks flush. "Thanks, but I've already reserved a room. My department agreed to cover the cost."

"Well, you can at least join me for a brandy by a blazing fire. That's a New England tradition."

The picture he painted sounded seductive. "Thank you. If there's time."

"We'll make time."

We'll make time. Was inviting women to stay with him and drink brandy by a fire something he did regularly? His invitation had great allure, appealed to her female side, so often ignored. She took a deep breath, wondered if he had an open marriage. Well, that was his business. Yet, no matter how he lived his life, she couldn't forget he was married.

And, to be fair, it wasn't just about Mark. She had her life with Dan to consider. They were partners, perhaps not as close or romantic as she'd like, but together nonetheless. That was where she needed to put her energy, not into a flirtation.

Chapter 5

The next three weeks were busy with g.e. issues still consuming much of Jen's time, as she had become the spokesperson for the task force proposal. In a flash, the Bennington weekend was upon her. Mark was going to pick her up at the subway stop at 96th and Broadway for the three-hour drive to Vermont. On Friday at 2 p.m., when she labored up the subway steps to street level with her pack strapped to her back, his SUV was already idling on the corner. He greeted her and threw her pack in the back.

Clad in jeans and a leather jacket, she was ready for the countryside. She climbed into the car. "Quite a large suburban vehicle for a city boy."

"It's lousy for city parking, but I like to camp. I can easily fit my gear in here."

"Where do you and your wife go?"

"I usually go alone. Barbara lost interest in the great outdoors when she started law school. Actually, she was never that keen on camping anyway."

He turned onto the West Side Highway. "I usually go to the Catskills or Green Mountains, occasionally, Maine." He turned to her. "You wanted to see leaves, right? We'll drive up the Taconic Parkway, which is more scenic than the interstate. Should arrive well before dinner."

The day was crystal clear and sunny. Jen settled in for a lovely drive. On the way up, they covered a lot of personal ground, including her years growing up in northern Virginia, his in Boulder, Colorado. She told him about her father abandoning her and her mother when she was twelve, her mother remarrying and starting a new family that absorbed all her attention and left Jen without real family. She threw herself into school, but it never made up for a missing mom.

They discovered things in common that were totally unexpected.

Jen, coming from a Jewish background, had a strong interest in Israel, not for religious but for cultural reasons, such as the clash between Israeli and Arab cultures the Middle East. The Middle East was a focus for Mark, providing compelling case studies of orthodoxy and secular modernism.

They also shared a fascination with immigration. She closely followed the effects of immigration on family structures and women's roles. He researched the processes of acculturation and assimilation, especially among Latinos immigrating to the U.S. in the previous hundred years.

As they approached Bennington College, Mark asked Jen if she'd mind swinging by the cottage he'd rented on VRBO so he could make sure he'd have access later. They pulled up to a charming stone house surrounded by fir trees. He picked up the front door keys left for him in the mailbox and checked out the interior while Jen waited in the car.

He soon came back, grinning, and hopped into the driver's seat. "All ready, including homemade bread in the fridge for breakfast and logs stacked in the fireplace waiting for a match."

"Sounds cozy."

He smirked. "A lot cozier than a dorm room."

"But you don't get to revisit your undergraduate years," she joked.

"Fine by me."

They drove onto the campus, a small, pleasant collection of stone buildings with maples and oaks lining the walkways and gentle hills rolling in the distance. One wing of the main dormitory had been emptied for weekend visitors. Jen found herself in a single room that looked much like her room at Vassar except for all the electronics – computer, printer, sound system, large screen television. Clearly not a scholarship student in residence.

She washed up, changed into slacks and headed to the dining room. She was pleased by the reception she got from a cluster of faculty members who knew her published work and were eager to hear about her current research. Members of the women's caucus accompanied her in to dinner and invited her to drink wine with them after their meal.

When the time came, the women retreated to the building's sitting room with a bottle of merlot. The evening flew by as they chatted about research activities and grant funds. Just as they were finishing their wine, Jen spotted Mark in the doorway motioning toward the parking lot. She excused herself, saying she needed something from the car, and said goodnight.

He reached across the front seat and opened the door for her. "A good evening?" he asked as she climbed in.

"Terrific. I see what you mean about the intimacy of a small gathering. Everyone was open and engaged with each other. I'm sure I'll stay in touch with them."

"I knew you'd like these folks. Are you ready for a brandy?"

She hesitated. "I don't know. Tomorrow's program starts early, and it's a full day."

He started the engine. "I guarantee you'll get a good night's sleep."

∼

Decorated with colonial-style furniture and red plaid fabric on the sofa and old-fashioned armchairs, the cottage lived up to its advertisement as "charming and homey." Mark asked Alexa to play Debussy's Clair de Lune and lit the fire. He poured two stiff brandies into crystal snifters and sat down beside Jen on the couch.

"Nice, isn't it?" he said.

"A major improvement over my dorm room. You chose well."

"I needed an inviting place to get to know you."

His comment was surprisingly intimate.

"We made a good start on the drive up."

"Oh, that was work. It didn't tell me much about you."

She shifted around to look at him head on. "That's who I am – work."

"And when you're dreaming? When you're lying in bed, reflecting on life? Where does your mind go?"

She laughed. "Sorry to disappoint you, but it's still work."

"I don't believe you, but I won't press."

They turned to watch the dancing fire. A log broke in two and sent out a shower of sparks. Mark rose and brushed the cinders back into the flames.

When he sat down again, he took Jen's hand. Feeling uncomfortable, she pulled it back, wrapped both hands around her snifter. "Mark, we need to level. What is it you want from me?"

He turned his gaze on her. "That's easy. A relationship."

"A relationship can mean many things," she responded. "In some ways, we already have a relationship."

"At the professional level. I'd like more than that."

"Anything more than that crosses too many red lines."

For what seemed a long time. he said nothing, simply stared. Finally, he said, "I'd like us to be friends, good friends, long-term friends. I admire you, enjoy you, would like you in my life."

She bit her lip. "You make it sound easy, but it's not."

"Look, I'm completely aware of the complications. We each have partners, busy lives, professional constraints. I'm not proposing an affair. Those come and go."

"Then what are you proposing?"

"Contact, whenever we want it and it works out for us both. Phone calls, emails, texts. Even physical contact, like now, on the rare occasion it's possible. Let's see how it goes and enjoy the moments we can be together."

He leaned over, rested his hand on the back of her neck and kissed her gently on the lips.

Before she could protest, he rose and said, "We'd better get you back to the dorm before your curfew."

He moved to the armchair, held up her jacket. She slipped her arms into it, pulling it together. As they walked out the door, he said, "How about another brandy? Tomorrow."

"Professor Anderson, I'll have to review my options," she said, mocking a serious tone.

They looked into each other's eyes and began laughing.

From her single bed in the dorm room, Jen stared at the ceiling, illuminated by a street lamp outside her window. She and Mark had moved fast, from consulting on curriculum to becoming part of each other's life in a matter of weeks.

She didn't know what to make of his overture. She didn't even know what to call it – a proposal, offer, proposition? Perhaps, invitation was best.

She was relieved he'd dismissed the notion of an affair. Much as she was drawn to him, she had no desire for a regular sexual liaison, certainly not one always on the sly.

Besides being rather sordid, it would be unfair to Dan. While her relationship with him worked on many levels, it lacked the magnetism she felt with Mark.

Yes, she was intrigued by the idea of sex on a special occasion, say, once a year at a history conference. She was drawn to the excitement of something new even if rare and within definite bounds. It had been fast, but they each seemed to have a gap in their lives that a new connection could fill.

As for the rest of Mark's invitation, friendship that went beyond collegiality, was personal but not intrusive, respected boundaries, that sounded quite appealing. They'd have to be sensitive to each other's commitments, never invade privacy or succumb to jealousy. She was sure she could do that. They needed to go over the ground rules, be sure they agreed before things went further. She rolled over, curled up, making herself as comfortable as possible on the thin student mattress, and smiled into her pillow.

Chapter 6

Panels, caucuses and discussion groups completely filled the next day. At the close of dinner, the Chair of the New England History Association, a Ugandan woman professor of African history from Wellesley, was scheduled to give a talk in the dining room. Mark passed Jen a note asking her to meet him in the parking lot right after the talk.

As soon as Jen walked out the front door, Mark pulled up in his SUV. She climbed into the front seat, carrying a tall stack of conference papers she placed carefully on the floor.

"Looks like you have your homework cut out for you," he joked.

"These are just the papers on women and family. There are a lot more papers on women's issues online."

"Sounds like you're glad you came."

"You bet. How'd it go for you?"

"Oh, the best part was the revolt against deconstructionism. Quite a debate."

"Are you part of the revolt?"

"Not necessarily, but I get where it's coming from."

They rode on in comfortable silence until Mark added, "In all honesty, the best part of the visit so far was drinking brandy with you."

She looked at him. "For me, an unexpected bonus."

They pulled up to the cottage, stopped in the hall to leave their jackets. Mark hung Jen's jacket on a hook then grasped her shoulders. He pulled her towards him and into his arms. "I've been thinking about holding you all day."

She lay her head on his chest. "I confess I thought about us last night before falling asleep."

"So, you don't think only about work in bed."

She laughed. "I make exceptions. I needed to think about your… invitation."

He took her arm, led her to the sofa. "Tell me about it over a brandy." He pointed to the bar. "You pour. I'll make the fire."

A large fire crackled in the fireplace. They settled on the couch with their drinks. Jen was primed. "I'd like to go over our exchange from last night if it's okay with you."

"I'm in your hands."

She reviewed the proposals he'd made – communication not only as colleagues but also as friends, boundaries when it came to home life, time together when mutually possible and desirable. "It's not exactly traditional."

"And underneath our professorial garb, we're not exactly traditional people. I like that." He fixed his eyes on her. "Does it sound doable to you?"

"Well, I've never had such a relationship, but it does sound doable."

He put his arm around her, rested his chin on her head, "Let's give it a try."

"Yes."

He jumped up, saying, "We could get even cozier next to the fire." He crossed to a small room off the living room and lugged back a thick foam pad. "This is an extra bed for kids, but we can use it to sit closer to the flames."

He laid the pad on flagstones between the grate and the coffee table, kicked off his shoes and beckoned Jen to join him. Grinning, she unzipped her boots and unbuttoned her heavy cable cardigan. They were on the way to something physical, and, despite her previous reservations, she was willing. They lowered themselves onto the pad and reached for their snifters on the table behind them.

"I have a toast," she said. "To a long-term friendship."

"No matter where we are and whatever else is happening in our lives."

She swirled the brandy in her glass. "That's a big commitment to someone I barely know."

"Is that how it feels?"

"Oddly, I feel like I've known you a long time."

They clinked glasses and drank. He took their glasses and put them on the table. Their lips met, they embraced and soon were stretched out side by side on the pad. He began to unbutton her shirt. "I want to see you by firelight."

She slipped out of her shirt, removed her bra. He ran his hand over her breasts, hardening her nipples.

"Now you," she said, and he pulled off his turtleneck.

Touching skin to skin, they explored each other's curves, ridges, cavities with their mouths, caressing each other with their tongues. They gave themselves up to sensation and wanting more, they slid out of their pants, shorts and lingerie, and touched each other everywhere with hands then mouths.

"I want you now," he murmured. "You?"

"Yes, now."

He kneeled above her then slowly came into her. With faster thrusts, calling her name, he quickly brought her to climax then exploded himself.

Afterwards, side by side, breath slowed, he clasped her hand in his.

She looked into his green eyes. "You're no longer forbidden fruit."

"Not forbidden to you, although maybe hidden to everyone but us."

"The secret garden."

His face glowed. "Hidden away, but we each have the key."

Sunday brunch at the meeting was optional since faculty with longer drives home planned to leave early. Jen would have liked to stay for the brunch with some of her sister historians, but Mark was eager to get home. They made their farewells and set off.

After an hour or so, they decided to stop for breakfast. He headed for a quaint inn on the Hudson River near Chatham, New York. Their table had a lovely view. Sunlight glinted on the water and warmed maple and oak trees with remnants of gold and red leaves. They filled up on pancakes with blueberries.

After the rosy-cheeked waitress poured more coffee, Mark said, "I'd like to bring up our ground rules. I know we agreed on boundaries with regard to our home lives, but I'm afraid I have to break that one."

Jen couldn't believe it. She'd been feeling so secure with the rules they'd set. Now he wanted to change them? "Are you sure this is necessary?"

"Quite sure. I don't want you to think I've been holding out on anything. Best you hear this from me before you hear it elsewhere."

She studied her place mat, not wanting to show her dismay.

He tapped his fingers on the table. "Jen, Barbara is pregnant. Three months. The baby is due at the end of April."

She was incredulous. "You're telling me this now?"

"Barbara wanted to wait three months before we went public. She's ready now."

For Jen, suddenly everything they'd said and agreed on evaporated like air escaping from a punctured balloon. She could think of nothing to say. Finally, she muttered, "Congratulations. I didn't think I was 'public'..." She pushed out of her seat and strode out of the restaurant to the car, where he joined her. Not a word was exchanged until they got on the highway.

He cleared his throat. "I see you're upset. Can we talk?"

"There isn't much to talk about." She took a deep breath. "I was willing to have a friendship, as you put it, with a married man. I was never consulted about a relationship with a married man about to become a father. Yes, I stretched with the married man scenario because of what seemed special between us. I won't make that mistake again with an expectant father."

"Jen, objectively speaking, there's no difference. We can be friends, close friends, even lovers, given the right opportunity, despite my parental status. But if it doesn't work for you, I have to accept that, although with great regret." He sighed. "All I ask is that you give it some thought based on objective reality."

"My feelings don't play any role? Too subjective?"

"I didn't say that. Obviously, they matter. But I honestly believe we can have the kind of relationship we agreed to, even if I have a child."

She turned her head toward the window, didn't respond.

They passed the next two hours in silence, the scenery looking a lot more stark, barren even, than it had for Jen on the way up. She put on New York's classical music station.

Mark told her he would drop her in the Village, given all the extra material she was carrying. When they pulled up to her apartment building, she turned toward him and said, "You asked me to give our relationship some thought. I've been doing that. I'll keep doing that until I figure out what works for me."

"That's all I can ask."

They got out of the car. He handed her a shopping bag stuffed with academic papers and helped her hoist her backpack on her back. "To be continued, Jen."

"We'll see."

Chapter 7

In the next few days, Jen threw herself into work, in part to avoid thinking about Mark. She set up a series of individual interviews with honors students to get their feedback about the program and talk about their career goals. She also called together Macaulay's curriculum committee to discuss the coming year's seminar topics. For her evenings, she drew up a reading schedule for the papers she'd brought home from Bennington.

Still, each night, before she fell asleep, her mind veered toward Mark and her angry reaction to his coming fatherhood. She had to face facts. He'd shared the news of Barbara's pregnancy as a way of including her, not excluding her from his life. Truly, if she'd heard about it through the university gossip mill, she would have been enraged.

Then what made her so upset? His timing? Should he have said something before they made love? Yes, he should have, although, admittedly, she would probably have backed away. A sigh escaped her. That felt sad. At the time, making love had felt tender and right, given their strong attraction to each other.

She asked herself what was at the bottom of her disappointment. After all, it was normal for young couples to start families. Just because she'd decided against motherhood didn't mean everyone else should. It was a personal decision, one Mark and Barbara were completely free to make.

Still, in Jen's mind, it put entering into a relationship with Mark into a different category.

Apparently, not for Mark. Why did she feel differently? Was she jealous of their marriage? Did she think having children would bind Mark and Barbara in new ways? Of course, it would, but so what? Her goal wasn't to make Mark her partner. She had agreed to friendship, not partnership. That made his approach, even if he had a child, perfectly reasonable.

Yet, it didn't feel that way to her. What lay beneath the logic of it all that upset her about this new circumstance?

Reflecting on her own life, she recalled the years after her mother remarried and became a mother to two new children. Jen had been the old story, the product and reminder of an unhappy marriage. Her mother had essentially disappeared as her parent, leaving her to grow up on her own. The pain of that experience, however much she tried to get past it, still lay heavy on her heart.

She couldn't now accept being a part of another family triangle. Mark believed he could compartmentalize – his own family in one box, his friendship with Jen in another. Not so different from her mother with her first family in one box, closed and stuffed away on a shelf in her closet, her second family in a new box, open and consuming her full attention and feeling.

She rolled over onto her side, clutched a pillow close to her. How would she feel if their roles were reversed, if she were pregnant? She was certain she wouldn't seek a friendship that was close and long-term with a man outside her family. There was something unique, even sacred, about making a family, parenting, starting a new generation. That would keep her from straying. There was for her a boundary that came with parenting, more than with marriage, one she somehow couldn't cross.

Should she give Mark an explanation, a way to understand her thinking? What would he say? He'd probably fall back on "objectively speaking, having a baby makes no difference." Well, objectivity wasn't the answer for her in this, though it often worked just fine for her.

Better to keep her distance. No problem. They were on separate campuses, lived on opposite ends of Manhattan, went to different professional gatherings. If their paths did cross, they could be polite without being in a "friendship."

Jen felt she'd arrived at a good place. Mark had been an appealing side road on her path, a detour passing through lovely vistas and stunning scenery, but she needed, wanted to stay on course with her career and her life.

∼

The next day, when Jen got to her office, ready to tackle the day, she spotted a message from Mark in her inbox. She dreaded opening it, afraid he'd want to talk more, something she had no desire to do.

Instead, he'd sent a short note. *"You might be interested in this"* and an attachment. The attachment contained a website for the College Honors Mentorship Program, which she clicked on immediately. The program, offered by the American College on Education, consisted of matching experienced honors faculty with newly selected administrators to provide mentoring about the rewards and challenges of honors programs. Jen was interested. While familiar with Macaulay's operations, she knew little about other college programs and the ways they worked.

The program would be stimulating, plus it had the added benefit of providing a weekly change of scene. Her big question was which campus to apply for. The only two colleges within commuting distance of Manhattan were Temple University in Philadelphia and the University of Connecticut in Storrs. While Temple would be an easy commute by train, she was attracted to Storrs and its more rural setting in mid-Connecticut.

She reviewed the bios of the two prospective mentors. Temple's mentor was a middle-aged Jewish male from the Biology Department.

The University of Connecticut's mentor, Maddie Johnson, was an African American political scientist interested in Jen's areas of women and public policy. Jen guessed also that an African American might have a refreshing perspective on the role of honors at a public college.

That afternoon, Jen sat down with the mentorship application and wrote a heartfelt essay about why she thought Macaulay would benefit generally from the program and why Maddie Johnson would be a good match for her needs. A week later, she was thrilled to learn she'd been selected and assigned to Storrs.

The acceptance email was accompanied by a warm welcome message from Maddie Johnson. She suggested Jen rent a car for the two and-a-half hour drive from New York City and stay at the Nathan Hale Inn on campus which had a pool, jacuzzi and other amenities. She closed by inviting Jen to skype her so they could get to know each other virtually before they met in person.

∽

Jen skyped Maddie the next evening, and they had a long, pleasant exchange. Maddie described some research she was doing on child care policy. She revealed that Jen's interest in women's issues was one of the reasons she'd grabbed Jen out of the pool of applicants.

Maddie had worked in the honors program for five years, first, as director for several years, and, now, as student advisor, a role she loved. She asked Jen which particular aspects of the honors program interested her.

"Well, I'm still quite new at Macaulay, but already there's an issue much on my mind."

"Namely?"

"Our program content is directly linked to aspects of New York City life and culture. All our interdisciplinary seminars revolve around city themes. Not surprisingly, many of our honors students aspire to careers in the city."

"Sounds logical."

"The problem is they don't know how to choose from the vast array of opportunities out there. They get on one track and stay there."

"Hmmm." Maddie rested her chin on her hand. "Sounds like you need a more broadly-based internship program."

Jen nodded. "I agree, but I wonder how to set one up."

"Well, I happen to know something about that. We'll put that at the top of the agenda." She paused. "Now, for our first meeting in the flesh, I'm expecting you on January 18th. Are you planning to stay at the Nathan Hale?"

"It sounds wonderful, but a bit expensive."

"ACE is paying. Let me make your reservation. There's a corner room, same price, that's like a suite. I'll get that for you."

"It may be hard to get me back to the city."

"Oh, don't say that. You've got to go back so I can visit you there."

"Got it."

Jen got off skype, glowing. Maddie was warm, energetic, welcoming. Spring semester couldn't come soon enough.

She dashed off a quick thank you to Mark for suggesting she apply.

~ *1996* ~

Chapter 8

The steadily falling snow made driving difficult, but when Jen arrived at the University of Connecticut campus in Storrs, the sight took her breath away. The limbs of the trees were covered by glistening vanilla frosting, the campus grounds looked like layers of fluffy angel food cake. So different from New York City, its snow coated with grimy sludge. She followed Maddie's directions to the Humanities Complex, where one wing of the building was devoted to the Honors Program.

She found the Honors Corridor, still bearing holiday decorations. A sign on Maddie's office read Advising, Dr. Madelyn Johnson, in Gothic letters surrounded by gold and silver stars. Jen's knock generated a cheer from inside, then Maddie pulled open the door and threw her arms wide for a hug.

"How was the drive?" she asked as she hung Jen's winter coat on a coat rack.

"Challenging. I'm not keen on driving in snow, but this campus is a wonderland."

"It's lovely in all seasons. Wait 'til spring and the explosion of forsythia."

They sat on the cozy couch covered in blue gingham and chatted about the afternoon's schedule, which included an honors faculty meeting, where Jen would be introduced, a seminar class from a course on global warming, coffee with the honors director, a campus tour by car, and check-in at the Nathan Hale Inn.

"If you're up to it, we can have dinner at the inn. The food is good, New England-style if far from exotic."

"That sounds comforting, although I wouldn't mind a ten-minute power nap before dinner."

Maddie grinned. "Take an hour. I'll zip home to walk and feed my dog."

"And tomorrow's schedule?"

"Two more seminars to sit in on and a meeting with our curriculum committee on internships."

"Perfect. We're hitting the ground running."

"Well, we need some time to relax. If you're free, come to my house for dinner tomorrow night and leave Saturday morning."

"I'd love to, although I hate for you to fuss."

"No fuss. I love to cook, Caribbean style. Shrimp creole, already made, rice and beans. Spicy, okay?"

"Yes, ma'am. I'll bring white wine."

∼

As Jen drove to Maddie's home, five minutes from the campus, she thought back on her two days as a visitor at the university. She'd met faculty from many fields, all of whom seemed delighted to be teaching interdisciplinary seminars and for the same reasons as prevailed at Macaulay. The students were bright and creative, and faculty interacting with faculty from other disciplines made for a provocative learning experience.

For Jen, relating to the Storrs honors students took some adjustment. They were so white, Anglo-Saxon, middle class. For the most part, they came from suburban towns in the Northeast, had quite traditional aspirations – law, medicine or business – and looked forward to settling down soon after graduation. Quite homogeneous, not at all like her CUNY students.

Following directions, Jen located Maddie's house in an area of faculty homes, one quite like another, brick ranch-styles with bay windows and chimneys. The only thing that distinguished Maddie's house was a mailbox painted in the colors of a rainbow, which Jen assumed was a statement, even though Maddie had said nothing about sexual orientation.

Jen was carrying both a sauvignon blanc and chardonnay, not knowing Maddie's preference. When she passed Maddie the wine carrier, Maddie's response was, "Cool. We can get as looped as we like."

They sat in armchairs in front of a crackling fire that made Jen flash back to Bennington. She hadn't thought of the conference in some time and was surprised by a flood of good memories. Perhaps Father Time was blurring her discomfort with Mark.

Maddie plonked herself down in her armchair, stared out the bay window. "Winter doldrums for me, even with the pristine snow. How were your holidays?"

"Not terribly exciting. A few parties and lots of work."

"No travels?"

"Not really. My partner Dan went to Florida to visit his parents, but I declined. My parents are not in the picture, but I did visit a favorite aunt in D.C. for a couple of days. How about you?"

"I went to Boston to see family and friends. And I dreamt about the Caribbean, my favorite place. I don't go in winter 'cause it's too expensive. But every summer, off season, when it's hot, humid and cheap, I'm there."

She reached for the sauvignon blanc and poured two glasses. "Here's to Week One at Storrs. I'm eager for your impressions."

Jen raised her glass. "And I'm eager for your input." She took a swallow, glanced around at all the vivid paintings on the living room walls. "Haitian, I'm guessing."

"Indeed. You're one of only two people around here to recognize the art."

"Haitian primitives, shrimp creole, and Storrs, Connecticut. How do you make it in such a totally white American environment?"

Maddie let out a guffaw. "I had to adapt, and it took a while. Now, I treat this place as an anthropological case study of another culture." She took a gulp of her wine. "I'm sure you noticed my mailbox."

"How could I not?"

"So, imagine being a lesbian in Storrs. To have any social life, I have to drive a half hour away to Hartford."

"I can see why you want to visit New York. In my neighborhood there are more gay bars than straight."

"Paradise." They laughed. "I'm coming spring break."

Dinner was superb. Home-made ceviche, followed by spicy creole. They soon got through one bottle of wine, opened another.

Maddie seemed completely relaxed. "You know, all your references gave you high professional rankings, but no one told me you like to party."

"My references?"

"Yeah. I always make a few phone calls before accepting a mentee. I spoke to the honors dean who came before you, one of your colleagues from the History Department, and Mark Anderson from CUNY."

Jen's eyes flew open. "Mark?"

"Yup. Wasn't he the one who suggested the program to you?"

"Yes. Who, um, suggested him as a reference?"

"Your former dean. He said you worked on g.e. reform together. Mark gave you high marks. You should thank him."

"I will."

"You seemed surprised when I mentioned him."

"Oh. I was surprised because he never said anything about a reference." And for other reasons she didn't mention.

"Well, he thinks a lot of you, and I'm glad he steered you to the program."

After another hour and a cup of coffee, Jen thanked Maddie for a great evening and drove slowly and carefully back to the Inn. She was in a light-hearted mood, delighted her honors mentor could also be a friend.

As she hung up her clothes, she thought about Mark's role as a reference. He'd given her kudos, didn't seem to be holding any grudges. That was good. She didn't want to cut ties completely, just didn't want the intimacy he'd proposed. She smiled. Maybe now was a good time to start healing the breach. She'd send a thank you email which he'd get in the morning. She opened her laptop.

Mark: I just came from a delightful dinner with Maddie Johnson who told me you'd been a reference for Storrs. I hadn't known anything about references or I would have thanked you sooner. So, thank you for helping me get selected. It's going to be a good experience. Best, Jen

Ten minutes later, close to 11 p.m. on a Friday night, he responded.

Jen: I'm glad you and Maddie have clicked. Based on my conversation with her, I thought you would. I'm savoring a picture of you, snowflakes drifting down outside, a roaring fire inside. Cheers, Mark

A roaring fire. For a second time that evening, she flashed back to Bennington and felt warmth toward Mark.

Chapter 9

The following weeks kept Jen busy with her Thursday to Saturday trips to Connecticut on top of her Macaulay responsibilities. Nonetheless, based on what she had learned in Storrs about the university's internship program, she felt inspired to work out a whole new approach to Macaulay internships.

The Storrs program offered internships in either Hartford or Boston, 30 or 90 minutes from the campus respectively. Most students took a public bus; a few lucky ones had their own cars. From interviews with the students, Jen got the impression that interning in a new, urban environment with agencies across the political and cultural spectrum greatly expanded their aspirations.

How would the same sort of program affect the aspirations of Macaulay students? They definitely needed wider horizons than New York City agencies. She envisioned them working in two or three different environments each summer, including Albany, Boston, and, most of all, Washington. But a summer would involve money, lots of money. The students would have to earn enough to replace a summer job, and internships were rarely paid. In addition, they'd need funds for transportation, housing and food.

Jen consulted a few students on expenses and came up with a budget of $3000 per student, or $90,000 for 30 students, plus a summer salary for a faculty advisor. She strongly doubted the CUNY system would come up with $100,000 for an experimental summer program. Nonetheless, she wrote up a proposal describing the value of a summer internship program over what was currently offered.

She circulated her proposal to a few key faculty members at Macaulay along with a request for names of foundations that might be interested. To her surprise, she got a response from Mark, who had not been on her list, not even on her mind. In an email in mid-March he wrote: *I liked your internship proposal and have some thoughts about funding. Contact me if you want to know more.*

Jen smiled. Mark again in a helping role. She wrote back: *I'd love funding advice. Just curious, how did you find out about my proposal?*

I told you, he wrote back, *I stay on top of developments at Macaulay. Would a phone call about funding be too invasive?*

Please call.

Five minutes later, her phone rang.

"Hi. How are you?" he asked.

"Just fine. I'll be sorry when the mentoring program is over."

"Well, something good came out of it – an excellent internship proposal."

"With no way to cover the cost."

He cleared his throat. "I wouldn't be too sure." He went on to describe the philanthropic activities of George Soros' brother and sister-in-law, Paul and Daisy Soros, who were involved with programs for low income and immigrant students entering public service.

"Are these people you already know?" she asked.

"I don't, but they're gung-ho New Yorkers. Send them a proposal and I bet, if you invite them to meet some of your students, they'll come."

She laughed. "And they will have read my proposal beforehand."

"They're known to do their homework."

"Thanks. I'll let you know what happens." She hesitated, not wanting to get too personal, but aware a baby was coming soon. "If I recall correctly, fatherhood is on the near horizon."

"It can't come soon enough. Barbara complains constantly about the big bundle she's carrying. She's due in a couple of weeks."

"Well, best of luck. I hope it goes smoothly."

"Thanks. Good to talk to you."

Sighing, Jen leaned back in her chair. Mark was one of those people who networked for others without asking for anything in return. And the exchange about the baby went well enough. It was remarkable how time helped her put anger behind her.

⁓

The following week, on returning home from Connecticut, Jen learned from a letter that Paul and Daisy Soros were willing to meet with Macaulay students. Unfortunately, they had requested a meeting for the same week Jen would be making her last visit to Storrs. Maddie urged her to cut short her mentoring program and meet the Soros couple. She proposed to come to New York instead for their final session and to "commemorate it with a party" as soon as she'd submitted her final grades for the semester.

Googling Paul and Daisy Soros, Jen learned they were in their late forties, Hungarian immigrants committed to funding immigrant students for their graduate degrees. She pulled together a group of interns to meet them, making sure most of them were from immigrant families.

The meeting went famously. Paul and Daisy quickly picked up on Jen's main concerns. First, many of the students were eager to try internships other than working in the city's bureaucracy and were thrilled by the idea of interning outside New York City. As one Puerto Rican boy, dressed in black from head to toe, put it, "I'd do anything to get out of garbage truck scheduling."

Yet, a summer internship was out of the question. All the students needed summer jobs to help support their families. An African-American girl with a head full of braids remarked, "No summer pay, no formula for the babies." Paul and Daisy displayed full empathy.

After the meeting, Paul invited Jen to go for tea. A chauffeured silver Bentley took the three of them to the Plaza Hotel. Tea in the elegant salon with French provincial furnishings was preceded by a glass of champagne. Jen would have felt intimidated by the grandeur except that Paul and Daisy were warm and friendly.

After they had ordered tea, Paul said, "We want to support your proposal. We hope CUNY will expand the undergraduate intern experience for honors students."

Jen's eyes lit up. "I'm thrilled to hear that."

Daisy intervened. "Let me be the practical one. I usually am. We want the summer rotating internships to take hold, so we'll fund the program for three years. If, at the end of that time, CUNY agrees to pay half, we'll pay the other half indefinitely. What do you think?"

"I think, at least I hope, that, after three years, the program will be so valued, the university would be reluctant to drop it."

"And they can get it for half-price," Daisy chirped.

Paul tapped the table. "Sounds like a bargain to me."

Jen felt the need to talk brass tacks. "You realize that would be $50,000 a year indefinitely."

"That's why we have money, to give it away."

Tears welled in Jen's eyes. Even with the Bentley and the Plaza, this couple belonged up there with Pope Francis. They offered to have their driver take Jen home after dropping them off, but she felt more comfortable slogging home on the subway rather than arriving in the Village with a uniformed chauffeur.

Chapter 10

In mid-April, Mark sent a birth announcement by email to friends and colleagues across the university system: an eight-pound girl, easy delivery, Kathryn Anderson to Barbara, Kate to him. He added with proud exclamation points he was on full-time diaper and feeding duty while his wife studied for her second-year law exams.

Jen sent a note of congratulations along with a postscript telling Mark about the Soros funding. Like him, she would be on full-time duty over the summer managing interns since no one else at MaCaulay was willing to take on 30 students who had rotating assignments every month.

Thinking about the interns, she figured they'd need more supervision, both personal and professional, than she could supply long distance. She decided to make an appeal to CUNY graduates in Boston, Albany, and Washington to house interns in their homes. The response was gratifying. She got more offers than she needed, with many grads volunteering for the whole summer.

She wanted to return the money she'd save on housing to the Soros Foundation, but Paul and Daisy insisted she use it to help the interns. When she asked the students what they were most worried about financially, it turned out to be clothes. Few students had "business casual" clothing, so Jen gave each of them a hundred-dollar shopping allowance. This generated a huge amount of excitement as well as group shopping sprees. The students planned an afternoon coffee in the MaCaulay cafeteria to show off their new outfits. They invited their favorite faculty, and Jen arranged for the student photographer from the school's newspaper to take professional photos.

When Maddie heard about the coffee/fashion show, she insisted on coming to New York for the event coupled with her promised visit. Jen persuaded her to give a short talk on the challenges and rewards of an intern summer. She showed up with her hair in braids tied back behind her head. When Jen admired the look, Maddie complained she'd had to go all the way to New Haven to have the braiding done.

∽

Maddie did a brilliant job with her talk. She cited challenges of a government internship as occasional drudgery with boring tasks; possible sexual harassment in the office; long hours that cut into one's social life. The rewards were gathering ideas for academic research; making contact with officeholders and staff; identifying future career opportunities.

Without any hint to Jen, Maddie had gotten in touch with Mark. She'd been wanting to meet the well-known, intellectual historian and invited him to a dinner for the three of them.

Hearing about the date, Jen rolled her eyes, not sure she was ready for dinner with Mark, even with Maddie there. "I doubt he'll come. He's a full-time care-giver this summer."

Maddie laughed. "It's all arranged. He's bringing the baby."

"To dinner?"

"A Japanese restaurant near his house with cushions on the floor, perfect for settling in a two-month old."

∽

Tokyo Teriyaki had traditional décor, square tables at floor level and long rectangular pads for seating. Jen and Maddie removed their shoes, lowered themselves onto the pads, and swung their legs under the table.

"Leave it to Mark to find a place," Jen observed, "with infant accommodations."

"I don't envy the poor guy," Maddie responded, "but at least he'll be free once his wife's exams are over."

"That's not what I heard. She has a summer job at a prestigious law firm that pays incredibly well but matches pay with hours."

"Well, her salary will pay for a nanny."

"Except Mark's insists he'll do the child care until fall semester. He's trying to prove something. I'm not sure what."

A lovely young waitress in a peach-colored kimono brought a sake bottle and small cups to the table. Maddie winked at Jen. "Another reason he likes this place."

When Mark arrived, Jen and Maddie made all the expected glowing comments about the baby, after which Mark said with a laugh, "We're getting to be good friends. She adores me and fusses when her mother picks her up."

He lay the baby on a pad; she immediately fell sleep. "Let's hope she sleeps through the sashimi."

At first, conversation revolved around people Mark and Maddie knew in common. Then it turned to favorite restaurants in Connecticut which Mark had sampled when he was at Yale.

"Well, you can make the rounds again in November," Maddie said. "The New England History Association is meeting at Storrs."

"No way. It's scheduled for Colby College in Maine."

"It was moved," she explained, "due to construction at Colby. You'll have to come to my place for jambalaya."

"Twist my arm." Turning to Jen, he said, "I assume you're coming."

She felt herself flush, searched for an excuse but couldn't find one. "Depends on my workload."

"Oh, come on, Dean Jacobs. You can always clear a weekend."

Maddie chuckled. "Especially when you can stay with your mentor."

"And drink brandy at the Sycamore Inn, a big improvement over the Nathan Hale."

Drinking brandy hit a little too close to home. "I wasn't planning on going this year." She swung her legs up, pushed to her knees and stood. "Be right back."

When she returned to the table, Mark was feeding the baby and Maddie was filling their cups from a new bottle of sake.

To get past the previous conversation, Jen brought up the summer internship program. "Mark, you were so wise to refer me to the Soros Foundation, but," she said, grinning, "I may have gone too far with this program."

She described the hours it took to find student internships and housing. She was only halfway through the group and had only two weeks to finish up. Nonetheless, considering the placements she'd already secured, she felt a sense of pride.

Mark reached for a cloth and began to burp the baby on his shoulder. Things got messy and smelly. "Diaper time. I'd best take off." He handed the baby to Maddie and got up. "Thanks for dinner. Don't do too much damage this weekend."

"Oh, we will," Maddie exclaimed. "Great to meet you."

After he left, Maddie said, "We finish the sake and talk?"

"Sure." She poured two more cups. "What's up?"

"You and Mark."

"Meaning?"

"I announce this dinner and you get uneasy."

Jen shook her head. "I did not."

"And when he arrives, we do baby talk, chit chat, and I announce the history meeting in Storrs. He says to you, 'Come to Storrs.' I say, 'Come to Storrs.' And you flee to the bathroom. What's up?"

Jen lowered her face in her hands. Maddie reached over and patted her arm. "Sorry for pushing. It's obviously more than I thought."

Jen looked up, tears in her eyes. "I thought it was all behind me."

"Do you want to talk…or not? Either way is okay."

"I guess I want to talk. I'm not sure what to say."

Then for the next ten minutes, Jen recounted the weekend in Bennington, Mark's proposal for a deep and long-term friendship despite their personal commitments to others, despite his parenting.

"How does all that make you feel?" Maddie asked. "Really feel?"

Jen reached for her purse, took out a tissue, blew her nose. "Sad. Disappointed. When he told me Barbara was pregnant and he would soon be a father, I felt I had to pull back. It was like I was given a beautiful gift box. I opened the ribbons and paper, dug through the tissue paper, and found nothing inside."

Maddie sat silent, not saying a word.

"I tell you all this and you don't react."

"Do you want me to react?"

A long pause. "I guess I do."

Maddie retied her braids at her neck. "I think a part of you fell in love with him. He feels the same way. A part of him wants you in his life, and he's not pulling back."

Jen sighed. "We can't have each other in our lives."

Maddie drained her cup. "Maybe not as a traditional couple, but I imagine there's a way you could make it work."

"His way," Jen said wistfully.

"Maybe his way, maybe another way. Maybe you won't know for some time." She waved for the check. "Stop feeling sorry for yourself. He's married, a new dad, and he loves you. It's as simple—"

"And complicated as that."

When they got home, Jen said goodnight to Maddie and ran herself a bath, often the place where she did her best ruminating. As she filled the tub with orange-scented bubble bath, she reflected on Maddie's brilliant way of cutting to the chase. *A part of you fell in love with him.* Yes, true, despite all her rules, reservations about his family life, and attempts to distance herself from him.

Where did that leave her? Taking up where they left off? Not possible. Lowering the temperature, but not shutting off the burner? Or letting the pot simmer while searching for the right ingredients for the mix?

Jen scooped up a handful of bubbles, blew them across the tub water and watched them dissolve when they hit the surface. For sure, she had no perfect recipe for Mark. She was experimenting, trying different ingredients as she went along, hoping, as Maddie had promised, she'd find a way.

Chapter 11

The summer was even more hectic than Jen had anticipated. She'd been hoping that once she got all 30 students into their placements, there'd be a lull as they got accustomed to their new work routines and living arrangements.

That did not happen. Some of the students made new friends quickly, but others were in offices where no one reached out to them. They reported they were lonely, especially evenings and weekends. As for work, some students were given great assignments, while others, as Maddie had predicted, spent all their time doing boring tasks such as answering the phone or sending out form letters in response to mail from constituents.

Jen needed to visit Boston, Albany, and Washington to consult with her students, their office supervisors, and their residential hosts. She began in D.C., where she had the most interns. It was easy to help with socializing. She provided funds to the MaCaulay students for a coffee hour after work where they could bring their new friends as guests. Everyone mixed. Jen also met with the hosts of the lonely interns, explained the problem of their isolation, and got the hosts to take their interns on sightseeing excursions on weekends.

Her biggest problem was getting work supervisors, often recent college graduates themselves, to provide the bored MaCaulay interns more meaningful assignments. Overwhelmed by their own workloads, the supervisors insisted interns do the routine work in order to relieve themselves of the burden. As much as Jen pressed, they seemed unwilling to make any changes. She noted down those offices to avoid assigning students there in the future.

∽

When it came time to go to Boston, Jen stayed with Maddie in Storrs and took the bus to Boston for appointments. Maddie was devoting the summer to writing up her research on child care policy but made time to take Jen to her favorite haunts in Hartford, on Friday, to an Ethiopian restaurant with extremely spicy food, and on Saturday, to a lesbian bar and grill where Maddie seemed to know everyone.

She led Jen to a table. "They're all gossiping about Maddie's new date, wondering where I picked you up."

"Well, I hope that makes Dan jealous."

"Forget Dan. What about the other man in your life?"

"You mean Mark?"

"Who else?"

Jen thought back to the summer's emails with Mark, hers about the wrinkles in the internship program, his about the admirable feats of his infant daughter – long sleeps, smiles of recognition, hassle-free feedings and diaper changes. "Either he has taken to fatherhood quite well," she said, "or he has an extraordinary baby."

"Or both. What's he going to do in the fall?"

"He's starting to interview au pairs."

Maddie raised her eyebrow. "His wife plays no role in this?"

"He never mentions Barbara, but she must be around some of the time since he plays squash twice a week." Jen cocked her head. "Anyway, childrearing is not confined to the female gender. Just look at life on the kibbutz or in Scandinavia."

"Jen, my dear, the kibbutz has returned to the nuclear family with women doing most of the childrearing at home. And single Scandinavian women still do most of it as well. The state has replaced fathers with generous policies for housing and pre-school, but kids still need mothers." Maddie took a long swallow of beer. "What about Mark as, for lack of a better word, boyfriend?"

"We've had lunch with baby Kate a couple of times. She really is cute."

Maddie groaned. "That's not boyfriend."

Jen grabbed the menu.

Maddie pressed on. "Are you coming to Storrs for the history association meeting?"

Jen shrugged. "I'm getting a lot of pressure from my sister historians, but it wouldn't be easy with Mark there."

"I can't see in this light. Did you just blush?"

"Maddie, November's a long time away. Let me get through the summer first."

∽

Some leaves were still on the trees in November. Jen looked around. She'd seen the Storrs campus in the crisp white snow and with bright yellow forsythia blooming but never in the fall when the maples showered the ground with ruby leaves. Lovely in another way.

She parked next to the Humanities Building in order to join her friends for the Women's Caucus cocktail hour. It had been a full year since she'd seen most of them. While she'd been consumed by work for the MaCaulay summer internship, they'd been researching and writing. She felt a pull to get back to her own scholarly activities.

The caucus gathering in a large conference room was lively with women faculty downing cheap wine and chattering about their prospects for tenure and promotion. Jen located the small group primarily interested in immigration, mostly women with connections to Mexico and the

Caribbean, and felt envious they'd made strides studying immigrant women in the U.S. She had to get back to research. Well, that was why she was there, to be motivated by others to resume her work.

She caught sight of Mark at dinner, surrounded by admirers. He waved. She watched him whip his wallet out of a back pocket and draw out photos, undoubtedly baby pictures. She hoped he'd inspire other dads in his fan club to take on active childrearing roles.

After dinner, when Jen got back to Maddie's, she was ready for bed, exhausted by her drive to Connecticut and intense socializing. Maddie promised they'd catch up at brunch on Sunday.

"Not tomorrow night?" Jen asked.

"Oh, I made a date for a nightcap with Mark, the three of us at the Sycamore Inn."

"You didn't."

"I did. Don't worry. Just friends reconnecting."

Jen felt ambivalent. She was uncomfortable with the parallels to the year before. Nonetheless, she'd show up as Maddie had requested.

∽

True to its name, the Sycamore Inn was surrounded by towering trees with sturdy trunks, peeling gray and brown bark, and branches with huge leaves that spread across wide expanses. Jen parked and made her way to the Sycamore Bar which had walls and tables of grainy sycamore wood, patterned with beige and brown swirls and stripes. Mark was sitting at a table for two with a conference program before him.

"Hi," Jen said. "We need a bigger table."

"Actually, we don't. Maddie can't make it. Something came up. She said she'll see you for brunch tomorrow."

Maddie seemed to be scheming.

"What would you like?" he asked as Jen sat down. "A brandy?"

"A glass of red wine would be fine."

He signaled a waiter who came over for his order. "How's the conference going for you?" Mark asked.

"Good. It's made me eager to get back to my own research."

"I've had the same reaction. No more procrastination now that we have an au pair."

"Did I see you showing off photos of Kate?"

"You bet." He reached into his blazer pocket for his wallet and passed several photos over.

Jen smiled. "She's light-haired like her dad."

"We're waiting to see which parent she resembles."

The waiter served their drinks and they chatted about MaCaulay's summer internship. "I've got to find someone else to coordinate next summer. It takes far too much time."

"For too little money. You need to double the salary. I'm sure Paul and Daisy would be willing."

She sighed. "I hate asking them for anything more."

"Jen, another $10,000 is nothing to them, and it will free you up."

"I'm not good at asking."

"But when you ask, you succeed." He chuckled. "You got *me* in a minute."

Was he referring to the g.e. program or something more? "Who exactly got whom?"

He reached for her hand across the table. "It was mutual. I hope it still is. I want our friendship. Very much."

She didn't respond.

"What's wrong?" he asked.

"I don't like being set up. Maddie should mind her own business."

He rubbed his thumb over her palm. "I think she did us a great favor, whether or not she intended to."

"Oh, she intended to."

"Jen, I want to be someplace where I can hold you, where we can be just us."

"Us? Two people having an assignation?"

"Two people who care about each other and have a rare chance to show it, a chance that shouldn't be wasted."

She looked into his eyes. They held each other's gaze for a long time. "I'm tempted but unsure."

"Let me reassure you." He dropped his head, signed the check and rose. "I'll go up first. It's 202. One flight up and to the right."

∼

Jen entered the darkened room, and Mark swept her up in his arms, kissing her hair, neck, lips. Without speaking, they undressed and he led her to the bed. He pulled down the spread, climbed onto the sheet and reached for her.

Heart pounding, she followed and stretched out next to him. She stroked parts of him she'd touched only once but had secured in her mind. She remembered him vividly.

"Let's make it last as long as we can," he said.

"At least until next year."

∼

When Jen had let herself into Maddie's house late that evening, she'd found a note taped to her bedroom door saying, "French crepes and crisp bacon for breakfast."

At nine in the morning, the smell of bacon lured her in her bathrobe to the kitchen.

"Sorry about last night," Maddie said as she transferred strips of bacon from her frying pan to a paper towel on the counter.

"I'm not."

"Thank God. Pour yourself some juice and coffee and tell me what you like on your crepes, either butter and powdered sugar or syrup."

"To decide, I have to try one of each."

"Feisty this morning, aren't we? What time are you leaving?"

"I've got to get back to finish my internship report for the chancellor. And I've got a problem."

"Namely?"

"The internship program consumed my whole summer. I don't want to devote another summer to interns."

"So, get someone else."

"Look, even if we double the salary, no one in the CUNY system will bite. I can't think of anyone who'd take this job."

"I can."

"Who?"

"Me."

Jen's mouth dropped open. "Are you serious?"

"Why not? A paid summer in New York, staying rent-free with my dear friend Jen, supervising honors students whom I love, and enjoying the delights of your neighborhood. Sounds pretty good to me."

"You'd have to travel to their various work—"

Maddie poured batter for the crepes. "No problem. It'll give you a break from me."

"Maddie, this sounds terrific. Since the Soros Foundation picks up the bills, there shouldn't be a problem in hiring you. You've made my day."

"A mimosa to celebrate?"

Jen gave her a thumbs-down. "I'm driving. Raincheck."

"Okay. Now you get yourself off to New York and into your research."

"First, I've got to shop and make dinner for Dan."

"The other boyfriend." Maddie grinned. "Have fun."

~ 1997 ~

Chapter 12

Dan persuaded Jen to join him the week between Christmas and New Year's on a two-day visit to his parents in Fort Lauderdale. To make the trip more enticing, he added a few days for them in Nassau. While Jen was eager to move forward with her research, a few days in the Bahamian sun was definitely appealing.

Plus, she enjoyed Dan's company, his wit and attentiveness, when he was away from the demands of his law firm. In Nassau, they stayed at a charming colonial-style inn and toured the island on motorbikes, flying back to New York on New Year's Day when the planes had a few free seats.

As soon as the new semester started, Jen gathered the interns for the coming summer and oriented them on how to identify and apply for jobs. There was a surprising call for foreign policy positions, particularly Middle East policy, as students took strident positions for or against Israel, the PLO and Hamas. Fearful the extremism of some of her students would antagonize staff in congressional offices or the State Department, she sought advice from Mark as well as others knowledgeable about Israeli-Palestinian relations.

"That's a tough one," Mark said on the phone. "I can give you some articles that are balanced assessments of the various sides."

"Is that enough to cool the students' tempers?"

"Probably not. They need to do more than read. Could you arrange a debate?"

"To reinforce the views they already hold?"

He chuckled. "It would if they debated from their own viewpoints, but if you gave them the other side…"

"Good heavens. Pro-Palestinian students arguing the Israeli case and vice versa?"

"Why not? That could be quite educational. If you can arrange such a debate, I'll be happy to moderate. I was a star debater at Yale."

"When, I'm sure, you always won," she only half-joked. "Mark, the whole idea sounds crazy, but let me think about it." She took a deep breath. "I also need to talk to some people here. I'll get back to you."

The more Jen thought about it, the more she liked it. A debate would offer the kind of stimulation and learning experience MaCaulay was supposed to provide. When she consulted her faculty, they were generally positive, especially when they heard Mark Anderson would moderate. That role felt too risky for any of them.

Jen scheduled the debate for the Friday before the start of spring break. She figured it would be good for everyone afterward to have a week of vacation to cool off. One of Jen's colleagues contacted a *New York Times* journalist, who jumped at the chance to cover the debate. Jen worried a reporter might either intimidate or incite the debaters. When Jen asked the debaters how they felt, they all promised to remain professional on the stage – no histrionics.

On the last Friday of March, MaCaulay's auditorium was packed, blue curtains parted on the stage, students studying their notes at tables across from each other. When Jen looked out at the audience, she could tell the Jewish students were clustered together while the African Americans and Puerto Ricans had huddled together on the other side of the room.

She introduced Mark and the debaters, all of whom were cheered. Mark explained the ground rules – no booing, shouting, catcalls; complete decorum or exit from the auditorium. No applause except at the conclusion of the debate.

Jen felt anxious. She trusted her students, but one spark could ignite the crowd. Mark would be masterful, but he was accustomed to adoring undergrads and grad students, not high-octane teenagers.

In fact, the debate remained courteous and controlled for over an hour. At the end of the rebuttals, cards were passed out to members of the audience on which they could vote for the winning side and the best debater. The winners would be disclosed right after spring break. When Jen asked for a round of applause for the debaters, all the pent-up feelings in the room dissolved into clapping and cheers.

Jen spotted the *New York Times* journalist, who came late and sat down inconspicuously at the back of the auditorium. When the room emptied, he stepped forward, introduced himself, and indicated he had enough material to make a good story. He congratulated Jen on assigning the debaters roles they personally did not favor and asked if he could interview a couple of the students.

She replied nervously, "I propose a deal. I'll give you some phone numbers if you promise *not* to publish the debate results. I want to keep those in our school. We don't want to set off any bush fires in the city."

"I'll abide faithfully by your rules. Frankly, I hope it's a tie."

∽

Jen was relieved when she totaled the votes. Israel won but only by a few votes, and a student representing Palestine won as best debater. Essentially, a tie. She sent out a memo to her faculty, encouraging them to discuss the results in their seminars but not go public.

To show her appreciation to Mark for making the debate happen, she invited him for a drink. They decided on the same wine bar, Beaujolais, where they'd had their first encounter. She brought along a copy of his latest book on post-modernism for a dedication.

"You really plan to read that thing? It's rather dense," he said as he pulled out her chair.

"Absolutely, although I'm waiting until the summer when I have more peace of mind."

"Good thought. And it was clever of you to assign the internship program to Maddie."

"She volunteered," Jen protested.

He flashed a grin. "And you reluctantly accepted."

They chose four different reds to taste, cabernet francs and *petite sirahs*.

"So, now that you've got an au pair, what do you plan to do this summer?" she asked. "Some of that camping and hiking you profess to love?"

He shifted around in his chair. "Actually, I've been wanting to tell you this myself before you hear from the grapevine."

"Uh-oh." She distinctly remembered the last time he'd rushed to beat the grapevine. "Another child?"

"Ha! I wish. Unfortunately, Barbara is totally committed to launching her legal career."

"Then what? A MacArthur grant?" She actually thought Mark was just the type of candidate the MacArthur Foundation would select for a half million dollar, no-holds-barred, creativity grant.

Sipping his first cabernet, Mark murmured, "Almost as good as MacArthur. I'm going to Stanford."

"A conference?"

"To teach."

"Summer school?"

"Permanently."

Jen was stunned. Leaving CUNY? Moving to California? She'd become accustomed to having Mark in her life, even if on the fringes. She loved knowing he was there when she confronted issues that puzzled her. She loved having a close friend just a phone call away.

He pushed his hair off his forehead. "They made me an offer I couldn't refuse. Full professor, teaching only two quarters a year, a part-time research assistant."

"Amazing. Congratulations…although I can't imagine this place without you."

"You were doing just fine before you met me."

She lowered her head, studied her placemat, not wanting to show her emotion. "Things will change for us."

He reached for her hand. "Jen, email and phone lines extend all the way to Palo Alto. We'll just have to calculate time zones."

She squeezed his hand but had no words. Bottom line, he was leaving.

"I'll even come back for the New England History Association as long as you're going. Come on, try this second cabernet." He held his glass to the light to study the wine's color.

"What about Barbara?"

"Happily, she found the job she's been dreaming of with an all-women firm that does only sex discrimination cases. She'll be commuting to San Francisco."

"And Kate?"

"She's coming with us," he joked. "So's the au pair. She'll take some community college classes."

She sighed. "So, it's all worked out."

"All except housing. I'll be house-hunting while Barbara studies for the California Bar Exam."

"Mark, I need time to digest your news. It's a…shock."

"Jen, I wanted to tell you sooner."

"But you waited until it was a done deal," she said.

"I waited until we were one-on-one." He paused. "You're what I'll miss most about New York, but our friendship will weather my move."

"I hope you're right." She wasn't at all sure about that, but smiled. "Let's get into the *petite sirah*."

~ 1997 – 2000 ~

Chapter 13

For Jen, over the next three years, little changed on the outside, yet everything changed inside. Although MaCaulay remained the most appealing academic niche for her in the CUNY system, the honors program began to feel repetitive, not to the students or the rotating faculty, but to the dean. Likewise, research on women in the U.S had lost its novelty. Everyone was doing it. The women's caucus in the American History Association had grown so large it put on its own conference. Finally, Greenwich Village was becoming more and more gentrified and costly. It lost its originality.

At a personal level, her life also remained in a predictable pattern. Dan, even after he made senior partner, perhaps because he made senior partner, worked longer hours than ever. Jen gave up on waiting for him to free time for travel. Instead, she began exploring the world on her own with an overseas volunteer group that combined ten days of volunteering in developing countries with ten days of sightseeing. Those trips were the bright moments in her life.

Even her relationship with Mark fell into a kind of routine – occasional calls or emails, part newsy, part personal, although the one thing they never spoke about was their domestic life. Their relationships with their partners remained discrete. The one weekend a year they met, the New England

History Association Meeting, remained special, two nights together with fun excursions into the countryside. It was the only time their friendship was tinged with romance, times Jen treasured despite their rareness.

She began thinking about ways to jazz up her life. She was clear on what she'd be leaving, but not on what she was seeking. When Maddie pushed her to attend a meeting of honors colleges in Washington, D.C., she figured a long winey dinner with her dear friend would provide the time and place to share her troubles and hash out possible solutions.

~

For a special dinner in D.C., Jen took Maddie to Bon Appetit, a small bistro on Capitol Hill with a gourmet menu, alcoves curtained in red velvet for privacy, and service that was leisurely enough to allow a long intimate meal.

"Wow, romantic," Maddie exclaimed as they sat down. "If any of my friends saw us here, they'd know we were in love."

Jen giggled. "A lot of engagements happen here, but I forgot the ring."

"But you do have something to propose. I can feel it."

"I do, but let's start with a glass of champagne."

"And snails, please, please?"

Jen signaled to the waiter. *"Deux champagnes et deux escargots."*

As they dug the snails out of their shells and sopped up the garlic butter with pieces of baguette, Jen recounted her general boredom with life. "Work, lifestyle, travel. Still, something is missing"

Maddie moved aside her plate of shells, clasped her hands together and rested them on the tablecloth. "Sounds like you need to make some changes."

"I agree, but what?"

"Well, let's start with what you love and how to bring more of that into your life."

"I don't *love* anything."

"Bullshit. Travel. Where are you going this summer?"

"Vietnam."

"To do what?"

"Teach English and see that fabulous country. But Maddie, that's an escape. That's not my real life."

"Why not?"

"You think I should take a job teaching English in Vietnam?"

"God, you're dense." She pushed away from the table, grabbed her purse. "You can order for me – the entrecote rare and *frites*, lots of *frites*. I'll be back."

Jen ordered their dinners and leaned back against her chair, eyes closed. Vietnam, teaching English? Where the hell was Maddie going?

Maddie re-took her seat. "As we were saying, you love to travel. Why not make travel your career?"

"Go into the travel business?"

"Why not?"

"Because I'm an academic. I've spent my whole life in the university world."

"Maybe it's time for a change."

The steaks came along with a huge basket of delicate *frites*. Maddie dug in. Jen stared at her plate, cogitating. University plus travel. Most four-year colleges, even those in the CUNY system, had overseas programs. Would she be happier teaching abroad?

"I repeat," Maddie said. "A change. Come up with anything?"

"Maddie, teaching abroad would be fun for one semester, but I wouldn't want to make a career out of it. Anyway, CUNY's programs are only in Europe. If I went overseas, I'd want to teach in developing countries."

"So, you have to go outside the system. Better start looking."

∽

The next morning Jen started looking. She cut out of the honors college conference and made her way to George Washington University, which had an extensive study abroad program. She introduced herself in the main office as a CUNY administrator interested in expanding CUNY offerings to developing countries.

The student assistant summoned the staff member in charge of Asia, Africa and Latin America. A grey-haired African-American came out, invited her into his office, and poured coffee. He gave her an extensive overview of the program he ran. "Too bad you're not job-hunting. My deputy for Africa is leaving next semester."

"Well, I could be inter—"

"But it's way below a dean's pay grade. I get it."

"Who would I talk to about getting into travel study?"

"The Dean, I guess. Kofi Winston. He's visiting our Asia programs at the moment, but he'll be back in a few weeks."

"Is he African?"

"Ghanaian. Here's his card."

"Thanks. I'll drop him a line." She rose. "I appreciate your time."

Later that day, when Jen told Maddie about GWU, Maddie also brought up the question of rank, telling Jen she couldn't go from being a dean to a deputy assistant.

"What if I made it a bigger job? I could develop new overseas programs, teach in the field, start exchange programs with African universities."

"Would you leave MaCaulay for that?"

"Well, it's only a dream, but, yes, I would."

∼

The dream would probably not have been realized anywhere other than George Washington University. GWU was a huge campus, rolling in funds, with a strong ambition to raise its rank among America's top universities. Jen had to figure out how to offer the administration something that would make GWU one of the best in the overseas study field.

She put together a wide-ranging proposal covering Africa programs for GWU students at new campuses, research activities for graduate students, and opportunities for African students to come to Washington. She sent her draft to Mark for his feedback. He praised it, even suggesting as a starting point a college in Uganda where he knew the president. Knowing GWU thought big, Jen didn't stint on funding. She even put herself in as a second dean, which would surely make the existing dean unhappy.

Not surprisingly, that was the only element of her proposal that made the university balk. GWU's President countered with an Associate Dean's job with promotion possibilities after three years. She grabbed it.

~

Moving to D.C. was a hassle. Jen wanted to live in Foggy Bottom, the university neighborhood, but the competition was intense since GWU students, many of whom came from well-off families, drove up the rental prices. She finally found a tiny brick townhouse in a row of nineteenth century houses that was a five-minute walk to her office. Although two floors, the townhouse was half the size of her Village apartment, obliging her to sell a lot of furniture. The lovely garden in the back happily made up for the cramped space.

GWU was willing to pay for a trip to Africa so Jen could familiarize herself with the African universities participating in her program. In the Fall, she was too busy learning her way around GWU to travel, but January, when D.C. was gray and cold, was a perfect time to take off for summer in southern Africa. She made her trip a month long so she could also visit several women's NGOs in preparation for a course she would teach the following year on women and development.

Jen got back to D.C. in time for the rush of students seeking advising for spring semester. She was shocked by how little the students knew about African life. For many of them, their semester abroad was mainly about learning African hip hop and taking luxurious safaris. Jen decided to require an orientation program for departing students to give them some idea of what they were getting into. The orientation, taught on Saturday mornings, put her on campus five and a half days a week, but it was worth it.

∽

In her Africa Abroad Orientation program, Jen tried to convey that a meaningful trip to Africa involved more than mixing with African elites. The students also needed exposure to the poor and uneducated, urban and rural.

As happened so often, she brought her dilemma to Mark.

"Jen, I get the problem," he said, "but it sounds like you want to offer a version of the Peace Corps. That's not what GW students are looking for."

"I agree. They couldn't handle two years as volunteers, but maybe two weeks?"

"My friend, the Peace Corps trains its members intensely before going. You could never do that."

No, but as she frowned at the noise students were making outside her office door, she came up with an idea.

"What if I could get students to spent a couple of weeks alongside a Peace Corps Volunteer? A kind of Peace Corps buddy?"

He grunted. "I see what you'd get out of it, but what would the Peace Corps get?"

"Ummm. How about money? GWU has plenty. We could make a contribution to each Peace Corps program our students visit."

He laughed. "Nice to be at a university with lots of money."

"Kind of like Stanford," she said drily.

∽

Dealing with the Peace Corps, Jen quickly discovered, was a lot more cumbersome than dealing with GWU. The bureaucratic process inched along. Finding the right person to talk to often took half a day. It took her a whole semester to get the Corps' Africa Division to agree to an "experimental" Buddy Program. The prospect of additional funds for village projects ultimately won the day.

Jen was asked to consult at the State Department with Nathan Perlstein, the head of USAID's Africa Desk. His office walls were papered with maps and photographs of construction projects in African villages. Perlstein, in a navy vee-neck sweater, looked more like a professor than a bureaucrat, tall, with curly gray hair, and a slim physique. He waved Jen to a chair, got up, and closed his office door.

He began by asking how she'd come up with the idea of Peace Corps Buddies. She described the GWU study abroad program, the type of privileged students she was dealing with, and her desire to have them experience something about development in addition to hip-hop.

He tapped a pencil on his desk then smiled. "I appreciate your motivation, Ms. Jacobs, but it won't work."

"Why not? Both the Peace Corps and GWU have agreed on an experiment."

"Unfortunately, the lawyers got into the act. GWU is now asking State for a liability agreement that if anything happens to the students – disease, accidents, violence – State is liable. We can't do that. The cost to the Peace Corps would be prohibitive."

Jen felt irritated, not with State, but with GWU. "The lawyers are being ridiculous. The students could just as well be in a car accident in downtown Nairobi or Johannesburg."

"True, but that's covered in the permission agreement signed by parents to the university. A Peace Corps incident is not. I've spoken to the GWU lawyers several times. They won't budge. Sorry."

She crossed her arms over her chest. "Then we end up offering the same Africa program as before. Nobody experiences anything about the 90 percent of Africa below the middle class."

"Not necessarily. I'm willing to offer an alternative."

Perlstein ran his fingers through his hair. He proposed that the GWU students intern for two weeks with the AID Mission in the country where they were studying. At the Mission they could learn about AID's projects and then make a few one-day trips to meet the grantees on the ground.

"And how is that different from my Peace Corps program?"

"The students will continue to live on campus, and, in the field, they'll be accompanied by adults."

She frowned. "Adult bureaucrats."

"That's the best I can do. I think they'd learn a lot. You'd be surprised how cool members of our staff can be. Why don't you think about it and let me know?"

"I will." She rose, shook his hand. "Thanks for coming up with an alternative."

∽

Jen pondered Perlstein's suggestion all Friday. She looked up AID projects in Africa and was pleased to discover an AID presence in 24 countries, including all the countries hosting her students. She also read through the bios of some AID overseas staff and found they were typically in their twenties or thirties, young enough to relate to her students. She decided she could, in good conscience, promote the AID field program.

She sent off an email to Perlstein. "After some research, I'm persuaded your alternative could be a growth experience for GWU students. I'll poll them tomorrow and let you know where the interested students will be based. I appreciate your help."

He replied, "Please contact my assistant, Betsy Stafford, with the assignments. Let us know at the end of fall semester how it all went."

Okay. The next day, Jen persuaded eleven students to sign up. It was a start.

∼

When, at the end of Spring semester, Jen reflected on her first year at GWU, she felt some pangs for what she'd left behind. A majority of her MaCauley students had been committed to learning and hard work; many of her GWU students were absorbed by social life and experiencing freedom from home. The GWU faculty were as impressive as the CUNY faculty, but many had cynical attitudes toward the students based on their privileged and spoiled behavior. Often, they seemed less committed to teaching than to their own research.

Jen had fewer pangs for what she'd left behind personally. In the beginning, feeling lonely, she'd missed Dan. Yet, neither of them made the effort to commute between New York and D.C. on the weekends. When winter vacation came around and they faced the decision of whether or not to get together, they confronted reality. If they hadn't made the effort on weekends, what was the point of trying to close the distance over the holidays? They agreed, in a friendly way, to go their separate ways.

On the plus side, Washington had expanded her horizons terrifically. She was working internationally, encouraged to build up her overseas study program, and had begun to make contacts in the nonprofit world of women and development.

Still, it was time for a change of scene. Working almost six days a week had given her an urge to break free of GWU and D.C. over the holiday. Global Helpers, the group she often traveled with, was conducting a trip to Guatemala where volunteers would tutor English. Then she would tour the highlands, visit villages around Lake Atitlan. A trip to Central America would expand her horizons even further.

Chapter 14

In mid-January, Jen spent ten days in Antigua, Guatemala's historic capital, tutoring English. She then visited Lake Atitlan for a week traveling around to the 12 indigenous villages circling the lake. The scenery, the lake and the volcanoes surrounding it, offered some of the most breathtaking views she'd ever seen. And the women's handicrafts, weaving and embroidery, were exquisite. She bought gorgeous caftans in brilliant colors for herself and Maddie.

Two weeks after she returned, Mark called to ask about her trip and she was thrilled to hear from him. She cast her eyes on the two woven placemats on her tiny dining table and the orange, yellow and blue embroidered pillows on her couch. They brought back fine memories. She raved on and on about the lake and mountains, promising to send photos.

She finally asked how he was doing.

"Life has been interesting, although not as breathtaking as your travels."

"Okay, out with the news."

"Well, it looks like Kate is going to have a sibling – um, I guess I should say siblings."

"What?"

"Barbara is pregnant with twins. They run on her side of the family."

"No!" Jen groaned. "You told me Barbara didn't want more children."

"True, and she's not too happy, but we made a deal. I do the child-rearing with, of course, the help of a nanny, and she hardly misses a beat."

Jen moved from her desk chair to stand at the glass door opening to her patio. "She'll keep her job in San Francisco?"

"Mostly. She persuaded her firm to open an office in Palo Alto, where she can work a few days a week."

"Are you moving? To make room for the nanny and twins?"

"Actually, I'm building an addition to our house."

Jen was blown away. She didn't know what to say.

"Are you still there?" he said.

"Yes, but speechless. I need to sit down." She collapsed on the small couch.

"No congratulations?"

"Is this what you want?" Dumb question. Mark's dedication to parenting was obvious.

"I love the idea of three kids. And the twins are boys."

"Identical or fraternal?"

"Most likely fraternal, but we won't know for sure 'til they're born in late summer. No New England Historical Association this year."

"I would think not," she muttered.

"Jen, this isn't going to change us. Take some time to get used to the idea. Our friendship goes on, as well as different stages of parenting." He took a deep breath. "I'll call next week. You'll be over your shock."

"Maybe. And, uh, congratulations."

She poured a glass of white wine, curled up on the couch, and closed her eyes. Twins. Even with a full-time nanny, twins took up time, much more time. What would that do to Mark's career? To Barbara's? Well, she thought caustically, the latter was no problem. Barbara had Mark to do the parenting.

She had to get over it. It wasn't her life.

The best way to distract herself was work. She moved to her desk and began to organize her class on women and development.

Before leaving for Guatemala, she'd submitted a course proposal to three departments for approval and cross-listing. Women's Studies and Anthropology had been no problem, but History, her home department, was balking, claiming the history portion of the course was skimpy. She understood their objection but had little time before school started in mid-August to bone up on African history.

What to do? Could she bring in lecturers or use films? She invited her colleague, Miriam Chebele, the department's African history expert, to lunch Sunday to discuss the problem.

∼

Washington was having a warm spell and Jen brought Miriam out to the garden for lunch. She'd turned on her outdoor heater and covered her round glass table with a red and blue Tanzanian tanga.

"We could almost be in Dar," Miriam crowed. "I should have worn something traditional."

"Next time. We have piri piri chicken for lunch with vegetable and peanut stew."

"You made all that?"

"Whole Foods helped. And we have South African wine. May I pour?"

They exchanged stories about their travels in Africa. A Nigerian, Miriam had mostly visited West Africa and was eager to go farther east and south. She had hoped to teach in the overseas study program, but the department wouldn't approve such a posting until she got tenure.

Over lunch, Jen shared her interest in women and development then brought up her difficulty in getting the History Department to approve her course.

"How much of the course is devoted to history?" Miriam asked.

"About a quarter. I'd be willing to stretch it to a third."

"Why don't you let me teach that third one time? Then you can just expand on what I've done."

Jen's mouth dropped open. "That would be fabulous, but I have no way to pay you."

"Don't worry. It won't take me any time at all. And," Miriam said, breaking into a wide grin, "you could return the favor."

"How?"

"You could put me on your list for teaching in Africa in two years when I have tenure."

"Done. Where do you want to go?"

"Capetown, second semester, when it's cold and damp here."

"You've got a deal. I hope the History Department buys this."

"Just tell them you want to learn African history from a real African."

They laughed and clasped hands.

∼

Over spring break, Maddie, seeking an infusion of urban life, invited herself to Jen's for a few days. During the day she hung out at the Library of Congress. Her second night in town she found a lesbian bar she liked in Northeast D.C. and told Jen she'd be out for a few evenings.

Wanting Maddie and Miriam to meet, Jen took them out for Ethiopian food one evening when Maddie was available. They went to a hole-in-the-wall on Wisconsin Avenue that had no liquor license. They grabbed a six-pack of beer in the store next door to soothe their palates from the liberal use of chilis. By the end of the evening, Maddie and Miriam had gotten so tight they began teasing Jen about missing out on blackness.

"There are black Jews," she countered.

"The Falash don't count," Maddie declared. "Israel only accepted them under pressure."

"No, I don't mean them. What about the Lemba in Zimbabwe?"

"The who?" Miriam cried.

"Guess you don't know everything about Africa." Jen described a Bantu ethnic group of about 50,000 people who had religious practices similar to those in Judaism.

"Jen, you do not have Bantu blood," Miriam said, laughing. "But Maddie and I will make you an honorary African so we can all hang out together."

The next morning, over coffee and muffins at the kitchen table, Maddie said, "This has been a wonderful visit." She wound a braid around her fingers. "Too bad we never found time to discuss the twins."

"Nothing to say. Mark's getting what he wants, more kids."

"And Barbara keeps him happy without having to be a mother."

Jen shrugged. "A curious relationship, but they seem to make it work."

"You're being remote. That's not like you." Maddie got up to refill her coffee cup. "Anyway, I'm not interested in their relationship. I wanna know how all this makes *you* feel."

"No strong feelings. Mark was right. I got over the shock, and I'm fine."

"Honey, we're talking about your boyfriend. Having more children puts him even farther away from you. You don't see it that way?"

Jen rubbed her hand over her forehead. "How much farther could he be? He lives in California. He sees me once a year, writes me emails, and occasionally calls. We remain good friends. Having three kids doesn't change any of that."

Maddie crossed her arms over her chest. "Stop me if I'm off base, but if I were you, I'd be sad he was closing the door even further."

She crossed her arms. "He closed the door a long time ago."

"Do you really believe that? I never thought so. I still don't."

"You're being a romantic." Jen glared at her. "Whether the door is closed or open a tiny crack doesn't matter. It's a distinction without a difference."

She got up, put her mug in the dishwasher and left the kitchen. Talking about Mark, his parenting, his distance, was frustrating. He lived his life the way he wanted. She needed to do the same.

Chapter 15

Summer for Jen was consumed by academic program planning and a trip with Global Helpers to Cuba. The Cubans were more interested in teaching the volunteers about their country than in sponsoring volunteer English lessons. That was fine with Jen who'd always been fascinated by Cuba. She loved seeing the society in the flesh and having conversations with remarkably open guides.

The fall semester brought some unexpected developments. The Namibia placements in the overseas study program took off as the three students placed in Windhoek emailed their friends and shared photographs. As for life on campus, Jen found Miriam's lectures in her women and development class absorbing. Outside of GWU, she got more and more into the world of nonprofits. She submitted several commentaries to foundation journals on the workings of NGOs in Africa, which drew considerable attention.

Jen was so busy she paid little attention to the big change in Mark's life, the arrival of the twins. He emailed that Peter and Michael were fraternal, healthy, handsome, and demanding, even with Conchita, a full-time nanny from Mexico who had worked with groups of children before and had no problem juggling two appetites and two sets of diapers. He reported he came home for lunch as often as possible, ostensibly to help out, but Jen sensed his home time was an excuse to immerse himself in parenting.

When Jen received a letter of inquiry from the Asia Foundation asking if she'd be interested in applying her African analysis to NGOs in Southeast Asia, she hesitated. She sought Maddie's opinion, guessing Maddie would encourage her to apply.

"Where would you be going?" Maddie asked.

"They've proposed July and August in Indonesia, Thailand, Laos and Vietnam."

Maddie shrieked. "They're paying you to go to Bali? Are you nuts? Get out your sarong."

"Not Bali, Surabaya."

"How far is that from Bali?"

"About an hour's flight."

"Fine. You work in …wherever…and I'll wait for you in Bali."

Jen laughed. "I haven't even accepted the offer and you're already there. You're supposed to be finishing a book this summer."

"I'll bring my laptop. Come on, Jen, this is a chance of a lifetime."

Jen leaned back on the couch, stared at the ceiling. "I know so little about Southeast Asia."

"What's to know? It's hot, the food is amazing, and it's—"

"Really hot."

∽

For Jen, Southeast Asia amounted to more than sarongs and snorkeling. Asian cultures and customs provided a vivid contrast to Africa although the underlying development issues were similar. In the course of her travels, she came across universities eager to host students from the U.S. and worked out an expanded study abroad program with placements in Indonesia, Singapore and Vietnam.

By the time the Fall semester was underway, Jen had happily expanded her workload with one foot in academia and one foot in D.C.'s nonprofit world. She assumed Mark would be too consumed with children to travel in November and was dumbfounded when he informed her he'd made a reservation for a ski cabin in White River Junction, New Hampshire, fifteen miles from Dartmouth, which was hosting the New England History Association. Delighted, she was curious to discover what the dad of three was now like. And, in all honesty, after two years apart, she was eager to spend time with him, even if just for a weekend.

***

Jen and Mark met up at Logan Airport in Boston and drove two hours to White River Junction. On the way there, they stopped at a supermarket and picked up steaks, salad, a baguette, cheese, wine and, of course, brandy. They got their professional news out of the way in the car so life at the cabin would be devoted to time as friends and lovers.

The ski cabin was no cabin but the third floor of a condo building overlooking a sea of fir trees. The décor was luxurious, the best part, a huge stone fireplace with logs in place ready to burn.

"Our five-year celebration," Mark proclaimed as he opened a pinot noir at the kitchen counter.

Jen reached for a plate to set out cheese and crackers. "Who'd have thought five years ago that you'd be in Palo Alto and I'd be in Washington?"

"And we'd meet in New Hampshire in November. Thank God for the New England—"

"History Association," she chimed in.

The sun sank below the hilltop, and they curled up on the green leather couch before the fireplace with their wine and cheese.

"What would we do without New England historians?" Jen said.

"Oh, we'd find historians somewhere, southwest or Midwest. Historians are prolific. The real question," he said, clasping her hand, "is what will *you* do when you stop being a historian?"

"Meaning?"

"You've gotten so involved in the nonprofit world, I keep expecting to hear about a career change."

She stared at the fire. "I've thought of it."

He leaned back against the couch, stretched out his legs. "It isn't written anywhere you have to be a historian. What's your ideal career?"

"Hmmm. Having my own consulting business, I guess, with a moderate number of clients. I'd visit their overseas projects from time to time. I'd expand from Africa to new regions to keep it interesting."

"So, go for it."

"Hah!" She threw up her hands. "Right now, I hardly have enough clients to pay the rent. I'd have to join a large foundation first to make contacts."

"So?"

"Mark, I'd be giving up tenure, overseas studies, all my job security."

"Maybe GW would give you a leave of absence."

"I doubt it, but it's worth thinking about. Dinner?"

He nodded and she got up to make the salad and ready the steaks for the grill. They ate by the living room window, light from a half moon softly illuminating trees outside.

He exhaled deeply. "Much as I like parenting, it's great to get away and revel in a night like this."

"Tell me about being the father of three."

He grinned. "Well, Conchita is making the twins bi-lingual. At a year old, they understand *si*, Miguel and Pedro. I lucked out in finding Conchita. She's loving, yet always in control."

"How do *you* do with control?"

"Pretty well. Barbara's the problem. She never gives them her undivided attention. When she's on the phone, they know they can wiggle away, start exploring, and make a mess."

"You're not worried about them while you're here?"

"Oh, a little. I'll call Conchita after dinner."

Conchita, Jen thought, not Barbara.

She did the dishes while Mark made his call. Afterward, he built up the fire, threw pillows on the floor in front of the fire screen, and grabbed the brandy bottle with two snifters.

"The best part of our tradition," he said, patting a pillow beside him. "It never gets old."

She laughed. "How could it once a year?"

"Complaining?"

"Nope." She kissed him under the ear. "We still have lots of New England to discover."

He took her snifter from her hand, set it on an end table, and pulled her closer. "Here's to this year in White River Junction."

～

Saturday morning, when they got to the meeting, no one mentioned them arriving together or choosing not to stay in one of the fraternity houses emptied for the weekend. The historians were either discreet or oblivious.

In any event, Jen and Mark both got warm receptions as they met up with their respective caucuses. Jen was asked to speak about running an overseas study program. Among other things, she recounted her rush to bone up on African history and the help she'd received from Miriam Chebele. She asked for volunteers who could help her with Asian history now that she was expanding into Southeast Asia.

Dinner and the talk by the Association Chair, a woman from Radcliffe, on family history were lively. Mark sent a hand signal about leaving at ten which allowed Jen to join her friends for a nightcap beforehand. When she and Mark eventually got back to the cabin, he proposed going right to pillow talk, trading time by the fireplace for a brandy in bed.

Once they were under the covers, he threw back the quilt and announced, "Before you seduce me, I have a gift if you have ten minutes to spare."

"I can do that."

"Then lie on your stomach. I'm going to give you a massage."

"How Californian."

"This is part of the package at my squash club. My masseur taught me the basics." He retrieved two bath towels and a small bottle from the bathroom. "I brought the oil. All you need to do is stretch out and close your eyes. Don't tense up."

"Isn't the massage supposed to relax me?"

"That's East Coast massage. This deep tissue massage invigorates. Climb onto the towels and try not to talk."

Jen succumbed to the minty smell of balsam and the feel of Mark's strong hands. It was just the way to end a day in which her mind had been zinging nonstop. When she rolled over onto her back, the massage went from stimulating to erotic, first for her, then, when she wound her arms around his neck, for them both.

Afterward, gasping, they lay back on the towels.

"I see why you like that squash club," Jen said.

"Don't get any nasty ideas. There's no masseuse. Melvin is a masseur." He nuzzled her ear. "And I'm not that Californian."

∼

Sunday morning, as they drove back to Boston for their flights home, Mark said, "Dr. Jacobs, I've been thinking."

"That's good. What's up?"

"It seems you're ready for a career shift. I've been reading your development articles in nonprofit newsletters and magazines. They're really good."

She turned away from the fir trees lining the road and looked at him. "How did you find them?"

"I follow you. I've got a development news feed on Google." He went on about the value of making her mark on developing countries. "I see you more as a practical analyst than a rarefied academician."

"Agreed, except I'm secure in academia and a newcomer in the nonprofit world. I have no idea where to begin."

He tapped his fingers on the steering wheel. "Just what I've been thinking about. Joy Sumner is a friend at the Ford Foundation in New York. She's quite involved with women's issues. Would you be interested in talking to her?"

This was so Mark. Every suggestion he made ended up making her life easier. She reached over to squeeze his thigh. "You're doing it again. Of course, I'd love to talk to her."

"Fine. I'll email her your info and let her take it from there."

"Mark, you're the *deus ex machina* of my life."

He puffed out his chest. "And I give a mean massage."

Chapter 16

Within a few days, Joy Sumner from Ford had made a date to see Jen when Joy was in D.C. over the weekend. Meeting at the crowded café of the Politics and Prose bookstore with normally high-brow customers pushing and shoving over weekend purchases, they tried to have a conversation about women and development. Eventually, Joy pushed white bangs off her forehead then reached for a manila envelope in her shoulder bag.

"Take a look at this." She handed over the envelope. "We have an Africa opening in women's health. You'd need to spend a considerable amount of time in Nairobi and travel around central and southern Africa."

"Not a problem."

"Well, check it out. If you decide to apply, the deadline is January 5."

"How long a commitment is it?"

"Two year minimum. Would GWU release you for that time?"

"I don't know. I have to speak to administration."

"Well, great to meet you," she said, getting up from her chair. "I hope it works out."

"I'll get back to you as soon as I can."

When Jen studied the Ford Foundation's job description, she discovered the issues she'd be dealing with were not the ones she'd anticipated. She wouldn't be focusing on agriculture, small business and micro-loans, her usual interests, but rather on reproductive health, AIDS, obstetric fistula, family planning. Of course, without health women had no chance at economic advancement. She decided to apply, both out of a desire to learn health issues and from a conviction Ford would bring her the NGO contacts she'd need in the future.

∼

Unfortunately, the Personnel Department at GWU was not at all receptive to her request for a two-year leave. The university did not want to assign anyone to the overseas study program on a temporary basis, nor did it wish to encumber a full-time position in the History Department while she was away.

Jen had mixed feelings about what to do. If she got the job at Ford, she'd be stepping into an ideal slot from which to launch a new career. She'd also be losing the job security that academics, in their heart of hearts, treasured as the best perquisite of university teaching. She wanted Maddie's advice, but suspected Maddie would push her toward consulting on women's issues in the nonprofit world.

To her surprise, it didn't turn out that way. She skyped Maddie that evening, found her, pencil behind her ear, crunched over a pile of student papers. Jen described the Ford Foundation job.

"And you want my opinion?" Maddie asked.

"Yes. Put yourself in my shoes."

"I could never be in your shoes. I'm a black lesbian with hard-earned tenure." She exhaled deeply. "No, I can't imagine giving it up – ever. You need to consider your options carefully."

"Hey, I understand your reluctance, but what about me?"

She reached for a coffee mug. "Listen, if you ever wanted to return to academia after a few years away, you'd find another job."

"What do you think about the two years away?"

"How would you feel if you didn't try for it?"

Jen took no time to answer. "I'd hate myself."

"So, go for it."

Jen sighed. "Thanks, Maddie, this helped."

"I'm gonna visit you in Nairobi."

She laughed. "I haven't got the job yet."

"When you get it. And I'll also visit Miriam's family in Nigeria."

∼

The Ford Foundation moved surprisingly quickly. Within a week of receiving Jen's application, the Africa Division invited her to New York for interviews. Before going, she absorbed as much as she could about women's health issues, but knew she was only scratching the surface.

The huge glass-fronted high-rise in Manhattan was intimidating. So much money, but mostly targeted to doing good. Her interview apparently went well because she was offered the consultancy by mid-February. While Ford wanted her to start immediately, she had to finish spring semester at GWU. When Miriam expressed interest in running the overseas program, Jen did everything she could to prepare her and was delighted when Miriam was appointed.

Jen was able to use her spring break for a familiarization trip, covered by Ford, to Kenya, Ethiopia and Tanzania. She focused on obstetric fistula, an appalling problem in sub-Saharan Africa where many women had difficult deliveries due both to young age and a lack of medical attention. With their uteruses or urinary tracts punctured during childbirth, they ended up leaking urine or feces all their lives.

Fortunately, there was a way to repair fistulas with surgery for about $500 each, which brought suffering women back to normal lives. While nonprofits in the U.S. and Europe supported African hospitals to perform fistula operations at no cost, few rural women knew about the possibility of repair or had the means to reach the hospitals.

Impressed by the skill of the hospitals performing surgery, Jen zeroed in outreach, namely, getting into rural areas and finding the desperate women, most of whom were outcasts in their own communities. The second step was education. Many rural people, ignorant about injury during childbirth, believed women with fistulas were cursed by evil spirits. Heartened by a hospital in Tanzania that had created outreach teams, called fistula ambassadors, Jen drew up a proposal for Ford to create outreach teams in all countries doing fistula surgery.

She left Africa completely energized, knowing her talents would be far better used in an advocacy role in the field than in a scholarly or administrative role at a university. When she got back to D.C., she sent Mark a warm letter of thanks for putting her in touch with Ford. He wrote back, cheering her on, but also expressing regret her new job and travels in Africa might get in the way of the New England History Association meeting. She bounced back with, "Find a reason to come to Nairobi."

∼

The next two years proved more fulfilling than any time she'd spent either at CUNY or GWU. She confirmed what she'd already suspected. Women's health was an integral aspect of women and development. Wherever AIDS prevention and treatment, family planning, and reproductive health were addressed, women were empowered for modern economic activity. Where women's health was not addressed, women were, at best, survivors.

The only thing Jen missed in her new occupation and lifestyle was contact with Mark. She managed to drop him a line occasionally, or have a phone conversation when in D.C., but her life and travel in Africa kept her ferociously busy and distant. Still, rare contact was better than no contact, and she and Mark both believed their friendship would survive her job with Ford.

Chapter 17

In March, during a leave for Jen in D.C., Mark asked for a good time to call at home. He never scheduled typically, just got on the line when he was in his university office and away from his kids' distractions. She suggested he call after her daily communications with Africa, say, after 6 p.m. EST on Thursday. She lounged on her couch in the living room, waiting, and watching the cold wind whip around the pots in her garden.

"Hi. How's it going?" he began.

"Well, I checked the national weather report," she said, "and it's 70 degrees and sunny in Palo Alto and a dreary 45 degrees here, so I trust *you're* doing well."

"Jen, don't torture yourself. There's almost never a time I won't have better weather, and March is a sure bet."

"Now that you've rubbed it in, how are you?"

"Pretty good, despite the changes."

"Okay, you got me. What changes?"

"Well, Barbara and I are experimenting with a trial separation."

She pushed up quickly to a sitting position. "What does that mean?"

"Long story. The short version is Barbara finds family life a major hindrance to what she wants to be doing."

Jen shook her head. "Between you and Conchita, she's probably never missed a day of work."

"True, but she hates having to catch a train home at the end of the day. She hates commuting. So, we're seeing if she's happier staying in the city."

She had a million questions to ask. But didn't. She wondered where Barbara was staying. Would she still see the children? How long had it all been going on? She didn't ask because she knew he'd tell her as much as he wanted her to know.

She did ask, "Has this been hard on you?"

"Not really. Conchita and I have our routine. It hasn't affected my schedule."

"And the kids?"

"They usually see Barbara Saturday or Sunday. And the twins have each other." He cleared his throat. "Tell me about Africa."

So that was it for then. She launched into the trials of working on family planning. Unlike Latin America where the churches, both Catholic and evangelical, opposed family planning, in Africa tradition was the problem. Rural farmers believed a large family meant more field workers, therefore more food and income.

"As you know," she said, "the opposite is true. Smaller families mean fewer mouths to feed, and more children getting educated and finding jobs when they leave school."

"So how do you do family planning?"

"Well, we never use those words." She put the phone on speaker, stretched out her arms in front of her, rotated her neck. "We call it family spacing, the need for several years between children for women's health. If the mothers accept that, they have only three or four children before they're ready to quit and come to us for contraceptive injections or long-term implants."

"Pretty tricky."

"Sadly, it works with only some women. The most rural and least educated still derive their status from being pregnant."

"Got it. How much longer will you be working on women's health?"

She sighed. "It will be two years this summer. I'm looking for something new. Maybe girls' education. We all know how much it changes girls' lives, but that's just what traditional villages are afraid of."

"You need a gimmick like family spacing."

Laughing, she said, "I need a few gimmicks, opportunities to try them out, and someone to fund a few projects. I'm writing a proposal. Maybe you'll read the draft?"

"You bet."

Once Jen had hung up, she sat, motionless, on the couch, trying to get a fix on Mark's separation. For as long as she'd known him, he'd avoided drama. At the same time, he was losing a partner of many years. He had to be deeply affected but he was keeping his pain to himself.

She looked out the sliding glass door to the garden. Heavy gray light but no rain yet. She pushed up, gathered her trench coat and umbrella, and left for a walk to clear her head.

She strode past the narrow brick homes in her neighborhood toward Kennedy Center and the Potomac. She thought again about her conversation with Mark. He'd conveyed the news about his separation in an almost chatty way. She'd asked only a few questions. It felt as if they were both avoiding something.

She crossed Virginia Avenue, climbed the low hill in front of Kennedy Center, and walked through the red-carpeted hallway to the huge statue of JFK's head towering over the hall in front of the three theaters. Despite all the gossip that had surfaced about Kennedy over the years, Jen had never stopped being an admirer of the ideals he'd championed, the appeals he'd made to the American people. He'd touched people's feelings, something she needed right then.

She stood for a while, deep in thought, feeling an ache she couldn't describe in words.

∽

Back home, as Jen hung up her coat, she heard her phone ring and reached into her coat pocket.

"You've heard the news?" Maddie shouted.

"I've been out for a walk. What news?"

"Your boyfriend won the National Book Award for his latest."

She was stunned, collapsed on the couch. "We spoke earlier and he said nothing."

Maddie groaned. "Modesty. Do you think he'll come east for the ceremony?"

Jen shook her head. "He's got three kids."

"He's also got a wife."

She hesitated. "Not exactly."

"What?" Maddie screeched.

"They've separated."

"Wait a minute. I need to sit."

Jen heard a chair scrape the floor.

"You said they're separated?"

"A trial separation."

"Oh my God. Do you know what this means?"

Jen took a deep breath. "I've been trying to figure it out."

"It means he's available. Amazing news."

"You are a foolish romantic. He is not available. He's a Stanford professor with three kids, a nanny, and a wife, not even an ex-wife."

"Come on."

She felt extremely uncomfortable. "Maddie, they're experimenting with separation. There's every reason for them to get back together. In fact, three reasons – Kate, Peter and Michael."

"The kids didn't stop her from taking a job and moving to San Francisco. I can't see Mark moving to the city with three kids and a nanny."

Jen didn't respond.

Maddie persisted. "Why are they splitting?"

"He didn't say and I didn't ask. Listen…" She paused. "Let's not beat this to death. I feel sad for Mark. It can't be easy. Let's leave it at that."

Maddie grunted. "I won't push any further, but you need to get real. What are your feelings for him after all this time? How are you going to—"

"To what? You want me to throw myself at him?"

"I want you to be honest with yourself."

"Goodbye, Maddie, I've got to go."

"Think, Jen, think."

Chapter 18

Jen had only two weeks before her final trip to Africa for Ford. In Africa, she would visit HIV/AIDS treatment centers funded either by Ford or the US government. She would assess the distribution of anti-retroviral medications for infected women and preventative drugs for high-risk women, like sex workers, who were likely to acquire and spread the disease.

She was also planning to meet with village chiefs over her proposed scheme to expand girls' education. Her approach was simple. Make a deal. Get them to commit to girls' completion of secondary school in exchange for a gift to the village – drinking water, electricity, a satellite dish. Of course, once she worked out the details of a package, she had to find a funder.

Time to turn to Mark. She found him in his office in mid-afternoon, just as she, on East Coast time, was ending her daily calls to Nairobi. "Hi. I'm back with another request. Before I leave for Nairobi, I'd like to pick your brain about funding for girls' education."

"Leaving so soon?"

"It's my last trip for Ford. I'll be back in a month."

"Perfect. I was going to suggest you come to Palo Alto when the quarter is over."

"Come to California?"

"Why not? Come see my digs, meet my kids, explore the California coast."

She moved from her desk to the couch. "Didn't you say Barbara came to see the kids on weekends?"

"Oh. Sorry. I'd better to catch you up."

Barbara had determined she wanted a major life change. The separation had morphed into divorce planning. It was quite easy, he said – mutual consent, fairly shared community property, visitation whenever Barbara requested. "The only thing I insisted on was full custody. I thought that might be a problem, but she agreed as long as she could have full visitation rights."

Jen leaned back on the couch. "What to say? I'm kind of blown away."

"Say you'll visit here between Ford and your next consultation."

"Uh, I'll think about it."

"Good. Now for your education funding, I have an idea."

She smiled. "You always do. Lay it on me."

"Gates."

"Mark, Bill Gates funds global health, eradication of disease, new pharmaceuticals, drug distribution."

"That's what *he* does, but he also funds what *she* does, which, for the most part, is women."

She scratched her head. "Go to Melinda Gates?"

"Why not?"

"How would I get in the door?"

"Well, you need to get her attention, but I'm sure she'd read a letter from the Ford Foundation."

"I'd have to sell them first."

"I bet you can do that."

Melinda Gates. It was a fine idea, one she wished she'd come up with. How many times in the last few years Mark had come through with an idea, contact, strategy for one of her projects? She had no problem figuring out how to approach Melinda Gates or present her a proposal in a compelling way, but she hadn't had the initial instinct. She'd been gifted with Mark for that. On the one hand, she was grateful for his help. On the other hand, she wanted to be autonomous, to move ahead by herself. She wasn't concerned about taking help from him as much lacking full autonomy. It was an aspect of her relationship with Mark as yet unresolved.

∽

In the next two weeks, to get ready for Africa, Jen made contact in D.C. with various NGOs working on women's health. She also spent much time polishing her proposal on girls' education. She couldn't complete it, however, until she'd spoken to a number of village chiefs. That would happen soon.

Lying on her bed, she realized she'd been avoiding Maddie. She didn't want to be cross-examined about Mark. The time had come, however, to call and say goodbye. She was apprehensive. As soon as she shared Mark's divorce and the invitation to California, Maddie would pounce.

As it happened, Maddie was quite restrained. She observed wisely that spending time with Mark now would be a good clue to what Jen wanted long-term.

Jen sat up, put a couple of pillows behind her. "Maddie, I've never even considered long-term. I haven't seen the guy in ages."

"All the more reason to go. He obviously wants to see you, be with you. You need to find out what's on his mind. You're not afraid, are you?"

"Not at all." She traced a pattern on the blue and lavender quilt with her fingers. "I'm…"

"Afraid. Listen, think about it in Nairobi."

"I'll hardly have time in Nairobi."

"Then think about it on the way home and, when you get back, hop on another plane to San Francisco."

∽

Fortunately, once she got back to Africa, the pieces of her education proposal fell quickly into place. After several visits with village chiefs, it became clear they were willing to deal. A well of knowledge for girls seemed acceptable in exchange for a well of water to satisfy village thirst. She finished her proposal and presented it to her male boss in Nairobi, who was always looking for new ideas. Since Jen wasn't asking for money, just an introduction to Melinda Gates, he wrote an enthusiastic endorsement letter and wished her a speedy return to Kenya.

She sent off her proposal to the Bill and Melinda Gates Foundation (BMGF). Once she'd combed the Web, she discovered BMGF had made a huge commitment to health internationally, and to education domestically, but it had not joined the two by supporting education overseas. She wondered if her proposal would fall through the cracks. To her surprise, she heard from BMGF within a week with an invitation to visit Seattle and present her ideas to Melinda's staff.

When she emailed Mark the news, he jumped on the travel bandwagon, insisting she swing by Palo Alto after Seattle. He would be done teaching, and June was a perfect time to enjoy the Bay Area. She had to admit she was curious about his California life. Even more, with New England no longer an annual event, they'd lose the special quality of their relationship if they never saw one another. It seemed to be time. She bought a ticket for Seattle then on to San Francisco.

Chapter 19

The Bill and Melinda Gates Foundation occupied a sleek, glass and steel, high-rise building in Seattle, large enough to house 1500 employees. Arriving an hour before her appointment, Jen used the time to make the rounds of the Visitor Center, an impressive interactive museum displaying the foundation's interests and accomplishments.

When she went up to the sixth floor for her appointment, she was escorted to a small conference room to meet two women staffers in their twenties who worked on African village development. Stacy, the more senior staffer, an African-American with braids wound around her head, asked Jen to summarize her proposal.

Stacy conceded that traditional rural attitudes were the main reason girls were pulled from school and married off at a young age. "The problem I see with your proposal," she said, "is the ground work. Who would find the villages, bargain with the chiefs, and arrange the deals?"

"Actually, I see myself as doing that along with an assistant I will hire in Nairobi."

"I thought you work on women's health for the Ford Foundation."

"Just finished that contract. I'm ready for something new."

"I see." She turned to her colleague, Ruth, a South African, obviously younger than Stacy. "What do you think?"

"The assistant will have to be male. The chiefs won't bargain with a woman."

Jen immediately agreed. "I plan to have a front man, so to speak."

"So, what role do you see for Gates?" Stacy asked.

"Funding the village projects. I'd take care of all the rest."

"You'll definitely have expenses – office, travel, communications. You realize Gates will not cover such things."

"I'm planning to set up a consulting firm in D.C. With Gates on board for the development of the villages, it will be a lot easier to raise funds for operating expenses."

"Maybe, maybe not." Stacy signaled to Ruth who rose and left the room. "She's going to get Melinda, who wants to say hello. Five minutes max."

Jen hadn't been expecting that. "Do I have time for the ladies' room?"

"Sure. The key's at the front desk."

∽

Melinda Gates, her long brown hair flowing over her shoulders, apologized for keeping Jen waiting.

"Heavens. I had no idea I'd get to meet you. It's an honor."

Gates laughed. "There's no honor in having money or even giving it away. The honor comes from doing something innovative. I read your proposal, and it's definitely innovative."

"Well, your staff has been quite helpful. They're definitely right I would need a male assistant for meetings with the chiefs."

She laughed. "Sometimes that's how I feel about Bill." She reached out her hand. "We'll get back to you soon."

Once Gates, escorted by Ruth, left the room, Stacy said, "You picked the right funder for your proposal. We don't do education *per se,* but we do work for women."

As Jen gathered her papers and purse, she once again sent a silent thank you to Mark for suggesting Melinda Gates.

~

Jen watched out her plane window in awe as the amber sun set over San Francisco Bay and her flight landed at the airport. As promised, Mark was waiting beyond security. He gave her a big hug, grabbed her carry-on bag. "Good flight?"

"Lovely. An incredible sunset."

"Your timing is perfect. By the time we get home, Conchita will have put them all to bed and you and I can have a nice quiet dinner."

"I was looking forward to mee—"

"Believe me, you'll have plenty of time with a six-year-old and two three-year-olds tomorrow." He guided her toward the parking garage. "How was Seattle?"

"Super. I actually met Melinda. As always, you had a great idea."

During their half-hour drive to Palo Alto, Jen caught Mark up on the conclusion of her work for Ford and her expectations for joining the nonprofit world as an independent consultant. "I get excited about the variety of possible jobs then I lose sleep over job security."

"Well, with Ford and Gates on your resume, you should attract a lot of customers."

"I haven't got Gates yet, but it sure would help." She faced him. "Now tell me about life as a Book Award winner."

"Ha! It would be a big deal at CUNY, but at Stanford they're a dime a dozen."

"I don't believe it. Too bad you can't get away for a book tour."

"Well, oddly enough, Barbara is taking the kids, and Conchita, of course, for a week in Lake Tahoe in July. So, I'm doing a week of appearances then and got Politics and Prose on the schedule."

"I hope I'm in town."

"Me, too."

He pulled off the freeway and crossed Palo Alto toward the foothills. They entered a neighborhood of contemporary, older, homes spread over sizeable lots. "It's a typical Eichler house, a bit dated but practical – lots of glass, clean lines, natural light." He grinned as he pulled into a curving driveway. "The best part is the combination of indoor/outdoor living."

"Very California. I love it."

"Well, it had to fit a growing family. No guest room, but I've got you on a guest bed in my study."

Jen relaxed immediately. She'd been feeling awkward about sleeping in the marital bed even if the female spouse was no longer in residence. She settled her things in the study while he set about serving dinner. The kitchen, at the back of the house, was glass on three sides and opened onto a large deck which held a wood table, chairs, and four Adirondack chairs in different colors.

"We're having fish tacos accompanied by Conchita's home-made taco sauce." He grinned. "I've become a pescatarian."

"That's also pretty California."

"A combination of health moves. Better for me, better for pigs and cows."

"But not fish."

"Yeah, the fish get a raw deal." He winked. "Bad pun."

They dug into the tacos and salad, washed down by a fruity Riesling. Mark proposed a program for Jen's visit – one day on the campus, one day at the beach with the kids, one day in San Francisco.

"Sounds lovely. I'm in your hands."

They finished the wine and he led Jen to the study. He held her in a long embrace. "I've been waiting for you to come here for a long time. I guess I can wait another night." He closed the blinds. "I hope the kids let you sleep."

"Don't worry. I'll sleep. I'm over jet lag." She kissed him on the lips. "Thanks for a yummy dinner despite the fate of the cod."

Chapter 20

In the morning, the kitchen was utter chaos with Kate screeching at the kitchen table and Michael and Peter running around until Conchita stuffed them in their high chairs, where they incessantly hammered their spoons and cups on the trays in front of them. Jen escaped to the garden with her coffee and sat quietly until Kate went off to day camp and the twins were banished to their own room.

Then she came in for breakfast. "A typical morning?" she asked Mark.

"'Fraid so."

"How do you take it?"

"Oh, they calm down in the course of the day. They're overexcited because of our visitor. You should see them at nap time. They're angels."

He put out fruit salad and yoghurt and refilled her coffee cup. "Ready for the campus tour?"

"You know, I was at Stanford about fifteen years ago for a meeting, but I'm sure it's changed."

"You won't recognize it."

He was right. Other than Palm Drive and the arched stucco arcade out front, the campus was one brand new building after another. Silicon Valley's patronage was revealed in every classroom complex, laboratory, and office cluster. Mark's office had a beautiful view of the campus from the fourth floor of the Humanities Building. They ended the tour at the Faculty Club, where they had a shrimp salad and glass of wine overlooking the sailboats cruising on Lake Lagunita.

After lunch, they swung by Whole Foods for salmon to grill for dinner. Not looking forward to getting back to Mark's, Jen was delighted to find Conchita had fed the twins and put them to bed. Only Kate was joining them for dinner. She asked Jen, "Will you read?"

"Sure. Why don't you choose a book?"

"No." Kate grabbed her hand and dragged her to the bookcase in her room. They looked over a collection of princess books, which Jen resisted, and settled on a book about a girl soccer player.

Back on the deck, Jen sat in an Adirondack chair, and Kate crawled into her lap. It was a warm scene, one that obviously made Mark happy by the smile on his face as he set up his grill. Over the salmon they talked about what they would do at the beach the next day. Apparently, Conchita had asked for the day off, so Jen would be playing babysitter alongside Mark. So much for a relaxing day. Still, she'd wanted to experience Mark's life, and so it would be.

⁓

The ride to the beach was full of shouting and bickering. Once they arrived, the kids bounded out of the car and down the path to the beach in an instant. Mark yelled at her to follow them and keep them away from the water. She charged down a sand dune after them and pulled them back from the waterline to the sand.

Mark finally showed up with blanket, pails and shovels. They set to work on drip castles, but the twins knocked them over before they were even a few inches high, which made Kate furious then tearful. They went for a walk, Mark continually shouting "away from the water." An hour of beach time was more than enough. Jen was relieved to get back in the car where, thankfully, the twins fell asleep.

At the end of the day, once Kate was in bed, Mark offered Jen a massage. Remembering New Hampshire fondly, she gladly accepted. They retreated to the study. After the massage, brandy led to making love, although not, for her, with the deep physical connection she'd felt in the past. Lying in bed afterward, she wondered about her loss of passion, suspecting her ardor was sapped by a surfeit of domesticity. She couldn't help but wonder if Barbara hadn't also felt home life got in the way of intimacy.

∽

For Jen, the best part of her visit was their next day in San Francisco. They visited two art museums, dined on dim sum in Chinatown, listened to jazz after dinner at a café in North Beach. On the drive back to Palo Alto, Mark, taking advantage of their high mood, asked, "Could you adapt to life in California?"

She looked over. "What do you mean?"

"Easy. We're both free now, which means we could be together." He took her hand on the seat.

"I wouldn't say you're free," she said pointedly.

"Listen, you'd have to live with the kids, but they'll be a lot more manageable in a couple of years."

"As long as you have Conchita."

"Unfortunately, she wants to leave in a year, but I can get an au pair." She had serious doubts an au pair could be anything like Conchita.

"So, about California?" he persisted.

"Are you asking if I'd move out here?"

"I'm asking if you'd come live with me."

She turned to look out the window. Living with Mark was something she'd ever imagined. Perhaps Maddie had romanticized the relationship that far, but she hadn't. He'd been married, then separated, now divorced but still the father of three. And while she still was bonded to him in many ways, she'd couldn't ever imagine anything permanent or full-time.

"What would I be to the kids?"

"Stepmother, aunt, friend, anything you like."

She didn't want to hurt him. She needed to move away from the kid issue. "Mark, you know I'm trying to start a consulting business. All my contacts are in D.C."

"There are lots of like-minded people out here. The Global Fund for Women is in San Francisco. The Gates Foundation is a hop away."

"Here is a lot farther from Africa than D.C."

He laughed. "But not Asia."

She sighed. "This is so out of the blue."

"Not for me. Look, I handled it poorly. Let me say it differently. I'd like to be with you full-time. I'd like you to join my family. I can't come to the East Coast, but you could come here. Think about it."

"I'm touched you brought it up. We've been good friends for a long time and—"

"Now we're free."

∼

As he said goodbye at the airport, Mark drew Jen into a long hug and murmured, once again, in her ear, "Think about it." He handed her the carry-on bag and joked, "Have a drink on the flight. You earned it."

"I did, and I will."

As she sipped her Bloody Mary on the plane, she tuned into the quiet hum, blessed the long, unencumbered time before her to de-brief. She rotated her head in a circle, realizing how stiff she'd been, possibly for the last four days. She was glad Mark had resisted pressing her. She needed time to think.

She had to ask herself if they were a natural match simply because they'd been good friends, and occasional lovers, for the past five, almost six, years. To him, being a couple was a natural step now they were both free. While she might worry about the impact of California on her career, he'd be ready, in his usual way, to work around that.

Anyway, her career wasn't the main dilemma. Not even the kids. There was something deeper, the question of how her identity would change by being Mark's partner. Face it. He would always be the dominant force, she the subordinate because his life choices – Stanford, California, parenting – would predominate, as would his personality, his attitude toward life. He would be the alpha to her beta.

Wow! Did she really believe that? She gulped down the last of her drink, asked the flight attendant for another. Head back against the seat, she closed her eyes. Could she have a truly equal partnership with Mark? How odd. These thoughts had never surfaced before, perhaps because the two of them had never been free to choose.

She stared out the window at the crests of mountains laced with the last of the winter's snow. She hardly saw them. Mark was uppermost in her mind. For all his wonderful qualities – openness, generosity, brilliance, humor, caring – she did believe he was, and would always be, the alpha.

Were all men like that? The issue had never come up with Dan, in large part because they'd never been ready to commit. And she'd had no other potential partners to compare to.

She pushed her pillow under her head and tried to nap, but sleep was impossible. At the back of her mind was her other big reservation, the children. She couldn't exclude them. She and Kate had started to bond. Kate had told her to come back soon. The twins were another matter. They were boys, they were younger. They'd be hard to bond with, no matter what.

Whatever their characteristics, these were three children needing love, attention, direction, advice. Say it, Jen. They needed live-in mothering, and she felt no desire to mother, no confidence she'd be good at it, no willingness — whether as stepmother, aunt or friend, as Mark had put it — to make such a commitment. She suddenly had a new, less judgmental, perspective on Barbara, seeing her not as a selfish deserter but as a woman who'd made a hard choice to walk away from intensive parenting to live her own life.

They were both different from Mark, who had longed for parenting and made the commitment. It was in his blood. And, despite the chaos of his household, he was good at it.

She'd have to level with him. Happily, he had not set any deadlines. *Think about it*. Well, she would do that until the time was right.

Chapter 21

Back in D.C., Jen had her work cut out for her. Finding nonprofits to fund girls' education in exchange for development projects would not be easy since nonprofits interested in one half of the deal – girls' education – had little interest in the other half – village wells, electricity, etc.

Her task was greatly eased when she heard from Melinda Gates that BMGF would fund development projects in ten villages on a trial basis. If Jen could make it work for ten villages, Melinda wrote, they'd consider doing more. Great. Now all Jen needed was funding for operations.

To get leads, she decided to go back to USAID. Why not start at the top? She made an appointment to see her former contact, Nathan Perlstein, the Africa Division Director, who had, years before, helped her with the overseas study field experiences.

Looking even more casual than before in khaki pants and rolled up shirtsleeves, Perlstein welcomed her back to his office. "I read your proposal. You do like to do things out of the box."

"Well, on this one, I'm halfway there. The Gates Foundation has agreed to fund the development segment. Now I've got to fund operations. I'll have expenses on the ground. And I need to hire an assistant, a male, to help me negotiate with the chiefs."

He nodded. "I concur on male. I'm glad you're realistic. The chiefs don't negotiate with females unless they're queens."

"I've never been mistaken for a queen."

He chuckled. "Well, funding operations, that's hard. Nonprofits won't like paying for operating expenses unless…"

"Unless?"

"Unless they're particularly keen on girls' education. Have you tried the American Association of University Women?"

"Why would they care about African girls?"

"They have an international division, and the director is devoted to Africa." He jotted down a name on a notepad. "You can tell Doris I referred you."

"Thanks. Do you think they might come up with $75,000?"

"Nope." He tapped his hand on his desk. "Maybe you can get them to pick up the salaries."

"The assistant?"

"Don't forget yourself unless you're doing this *pro bono*."

She liked his practicality. "Wish I could."

He stood, turned to look out his window at the small park across the street. "What's the name of your outfit?"

"Ummm. Haven't got one."

"Well, USAID can't help you until you're a 501c3."

"And if I were?"

"We might be able to give you a desk, phone and internet in the AID Mission in Nairobi, although I wouldn't want that spread around."

Practical, down-to-earth, yet encouraging. He'd raised her spirits enormously.

"I'll get a name and the paperwork going today," she said.

"Well, be original with the name. 'Sex,' 'gender,' 'empowerment' – they're overused. Come up with something novel." He chuckled. "You know how to do that."

She definitely liked the guy. He was someone she could talk to. And the offer of a Nairobi office and phone was a blessing. As she walked home, perspiring in the humid air along Pennsylvania Avenue, she thought about a name. She didn't want to focus on girls since her nonprofit would be used for other purposes in the future. She wanted to publicize her cooperation with villages. She mulled over different words – progress, development, advancement. How about Village Advancement? She liked it, texted Nathan with the name.

He came back immediately. "A bit dry. How about Village Advantage?" Wow! She loved it, texted back, "You got it!"

He replied, "Fine, but please leave my name out of it. No conflicts of interest!"

～

Jen spent the whole evening filling out forms to become a 501c3. Since she had to show some assets, she moved all her savings from the Ford Foundation into a Village Advantage checking account. Then she asked a good friend at the IRS to move her 501c3 application to the top of the list.

In the next few days, Jen called on Doris Jamison, a white-haired granny at AAUW, who was happy to meet her based on Nathan Perlstein's referral. Jen had prepared carefully for the meeting, trying to be as strategic as possible. She started out by waxing eloquently about the value of getting African girls through high school.

Jamison's eyes twinkled. "That's what AAUW is all about."

Jen next explained her need for funds to cover salaries and a small office in Nairobi.

"Oh, my dear, I'm so sorry but our organization doesn't fund operations."

She was ready for that. "I so hoped you'd respond positively. You'd be such a great partner for the Gates Foundation."

"Bill Gates?"

"Actually, Melinda Gates. She's funding the village part of the project."

Jen could see the lightbulb flick on in Jamison's mind.

"Well, well. Interesting. We'd love to partner with Melinda Gates. How much did you have in mind?"

"Not much. I'll find other funds for the office. So, I'd need $50,000 for my salary and an assistant. Melinda is probably good for five times that."

"Oh, my. Well, AAUW could probably do a small part, say, salaries."

Laying it on, Jen said, "I think that would make Melinda quite happy."

∼

Jen felt like skipping on her way home. She'd pulled it off and felt more confident about running her own consulting firm than ever before. Even better, she'd done it on her own, hadn't even brought it up with Mark. Time for her to spread her wings.

Jen's consulting firm, Village Advantage, Inc., was on the way to being launched. To celebrate, she called Maddie who, not surprisingly, came up with a party. She invited Jen to join a group of lesbians renting a house in Provincetown for a long weekend. "While you don't meet the membership requirements," Maddie teased, "I can vouch you're les-friendly."

"I'll wear lavender," Jen promised.

"My dear, that is so old. Get a rainbow tee shirt."

∼

Maddie picked Jen up at Boston's Logan Airport, and they sped to Provincetown, Cape Cod's gay oasis. The group of women had rented a white clapboard house on the beach with four bedrooms and a jacuzzi on a huge deck that overlooked the dunes. The women, Boston lawyers and bankers in their forties and fifties, were eager to hear about Jen's time in Africa. Over a spaghetti dinner on the deck, they heaved question after question at her.

"Well, I'm coming next time you go," Maddie said. "I'm not going to miss bargaining with a village chief."

"I'm not sure I'd want to be there for that one," one of the lawyers joked.

After dinner, in the light of a half moon, the women took a long walk on the beach. The setting was perfect except for raucous shouts from some of the houses as vacationers celebrated the end of summer.

∼

The next morning, Jen and Maddie got up at 6 a.m., made coffee, and decided to walk the beach in the opposite direction. Wrapped in fleeces against the early chill, they set off, mugs in hand, to enjoy the sunrise.

After a few minutes, Maddie said, "You know, you never really told me about California. Mostly, you talked about Melinda Gates."

"I did tell you. Stanford, the beach, San Francisco. I was there only four days."

"You know that's not what I mean. What about you and Mark?"

Jen hesitated. It was hard to explain to Maddie why she was letting an invitation for togetherness pass her by. Finally, she said, "You're going to jump on me."

"Try me."

She described as best she could how she felt about Mark's lifestyle as parent, homemaker, provider. He obviously had a strong commitment to maintaining his life the way it was.

"Understandable – three kids, no wife. He isn't about to go backpacking around the world."

"Yes, I understand that. And he did ask me to join him."

"What?" She stopped in her tracks. "So?"

"So, joining him feels like I'd be a supplement – not a complement – to what he already has. Do you understand?"

"Not really." She faced Jen. "Look, he knows he needs help with the kids. So, he gets help. He wants you to keep your career going. So, what's the problem?"

Jen looked down, stooped to pick up a large unbroken clam shell. "Look at this shell. It has two distinct halves which make a whole."

"Yeah—"

"Now imagine half of this shell. The other half is missing. You can pick up half a shell anywhere on this beach and stick it next to this one and it won't match. It will be a supplement."

Maddie stood, hands on her hips, shaking her head.

"The shell is how I feel about Mark," Jen continued. "I care about him, admire him, but I don't want to spend my life supplementing his."

"Jeez, I've gotta think about this one. You've had a close friendship for how many years?"

"Almost six."

They walked on in silence, turned around at the lifeguard station, and stopped to watch the sun peek above the horizon. Then they headed back to the house, Jen still clutching the clam shell. It wasn't a perfect analogy. Even when the shell was intact, as, say, it had been for Mark and Barbara, it didn't stick together. She tossed it in the cool sand.

Mark didn't need a matching shell. That's what *she* needed, someone whose shape and interests matched hers.

He needed a smaller shell that would fit inside his. Not her, not Barbara, but a docile shell seeking a place to nest. She wondered if he'd ever understand.

Chapter 22

The next month was extremely productive. Jen's application for nonprofit status was approved and Nathan delivered on his offer of office space and a phone line in Nairobi. With the help of Ford in Nairobi, she was able to identify three possible candidates for her assistant's job. By October she was ready to leave for Africa. She hated to miss Fall in D.C., the brisk, dry air, the startling colors, mums in every garden. Still, Nairobi would be pleasant, temperatures in the 70s, the tail end of the dry season.

She resumed her residence at a downtown Nairobi apartment complex for long-term visitors that was walking distance to the USAID Mission. The Mission staff were apparently used to having visitors occupying the extra office to conduct projects. They were intrigued by Jen's prospective dealings with the chiefs. She planned to test the waters with two chiefs she already knew from her work with Ford.

The candidates for the assistant's position were all well-educated and enthusiastic. Evidently, it was a coup for any one of them to get a foot in the door as a way to secure full-time employment with some agency from the U.S. Of the three candidates, she found herself leaning toward Thabiri, who was tall and very dark, in part because he had a Swahili name and in part because he spoke several local dialects.

At their second interview in her borrowed office, Jen asked him a string of questions. "Why are you interested in girls' education?" she began.

He tightened his tie made from wildly-colored local fabric. "Educated girls seek jobs rather than marrying and having children. They end up giving more to their own families, more to the community."

"Right. Is your mother educated?"

"No, but my wife graduated from university and works as an accountant. When we have children, they will stay in school until graduation."

"That's good." She looked at her notes. "Thabiri, in all honesty, what do you think of this project with the chiefs? What will make it work?"

He smiled, flashing startling white teeth. "Well, the first time you meet them, you need to give them a gift."

"Oh, I hadn't thought of that. What kind of gift?"

"Something high tech like a phone or a watch. I know places where we can get good quality at low prices."

"Good. What else?"

"We need to check out what the village needs. It's not always what the chief wants. We have to talk to the villagers first to find out."

Jen cocked her head. "I'm not sure what you mean."

"Well, the chief could say they need internet, but the women really want a well so they don't have to walk hours each day to the river. Or they want cookstoves so they can cook more safely with briquettes instead of wood."

"I hear you, but what if the chief insists on internet?"

"Then I think we have to find another village."

She smiled. "You're tough. I like that."

Thabiri laughed. "When the chief thinks you will go somewhere else, he will suddenly want cookstoves."

"What makes you think so?"

"My father was a chief."

That clinched it. She hired Thabiri, son-of-chief, and they began to draw up a schedule for village visits.

It took longer for Jen to complete deals with the village chiefs than she expected. The negotiation style was slow and each village required at least two visits. By the end of November, she had arranged only five deals, all in Kenya.

~

Jen returned to the States for December and the holidays, leaving Thabiri to make contacts with villages in Uganda and Tanzania for her return.

Mark surprised her with a dinner invitation in Washington in mid-December. He'd been asked to give a lecture at Georgetown University and proposed a late dinner afterwards at the Tabard Inn where he was staying. Although she knew the Inn's restaurant was noted for fine food, she wondered if meeting at his hotel wasn't also an invitation to end the evening in his room.

That evening, it poured. Unable to find a cab or Uber, she took the Metro and walked a few blocks, arriving drenched. The cozy cocktail lounge, once the living room of the brownstone building, was almost empty. She was able to relax in a wing chair next to the fireplace and sip a glass of burgundy while waiting for Mark. He arrived a bit late and less rain-washed than she had been. He explained that Georgetown had a limo available for his transportation. Posh. He escorted her to the dining room and, due to the late hour, they ordered immediately.

"How's deal-making going in Africa?" he asked.

"Not as quickly as I'd like. Lots of protocol. Fortunately, I have Thabiri to advise me. We have another five villages to go in Uganda and Tanzania."

"You know, I'm thinking of coming to visit."

"You what?"

"Me and Kate. She has a passion for animals. I thought I'd take her on a safari before the twins are older and insist on coming along. One of the safari companies I like is in Tanzania."

Jen had little interest in a family holiday, but a few days with Kate would probably work. "I couldn't take time off for a safari, but I could show you Zanzibar for a couple of days."

"That sounds terrific. My winter quarter ends in March. Will you be there then?"

"Yes. My plan is to finish up my project by then."

"Great. Let me see what I can put together."

Their dinner conversation was all impersonal – work now and in the future, kids and caretakers. Mark had located a French au pair couple to take over when Conchita moved back to Mexico.

"A couple? I never heard of that."

"They're rare but work well for large families. They cost only a bit more and Marie and Yves are keen on California."

"A male would be great for the twins."

"I'm not macho enough?" he joked.

"The twins don't need macho. They need someone who likes batting a ball around."

"True. Baseball was not one of my strengths."

Over coffee, Mark reached for her hand. "I've been thinking about your visit to Palo Alto. Sorry if I surprised you. Can we go back to just friends?"

"We can. You know I appreciate our friendship, even being friends with benefits."

"Whenever possible, like tonight." He put her hand to his mouth, kissed it. "I have a fireplace in my room."

She laughed. "You happened to get the one room in the inn with a fireplace?"

"Actually, there are two such rooms, but mine also has a bottle of brandy."

"So we revisit the past?"

"Why not? There's no rule book. If we want to be together, especially in a place as romantic as the Tabard Inn, we should be."

The attraction was still there. "I like it."

He waved for the check, signed it, and put his arm around her waist as they climbed the stairs to his room.

Chapter 23

The Global Studies Program at George Washington University had scheduled a workshop on education in the developing world. Jen was eager not only to hear the speakers, but also to meet others working for girls' education.

During the coffee break, she ran into Nathan Perlstein, who said, "Jennifer Jacobs, I'm not surprised to see you here."

She'd been wanting, for some time, to show her appreciation for his help with Village Advantage and invited him to lunch after the workshop. He accepted, and she took him to the sushi bar at the nearby Watergate Hotel.

"What did you think of the workshop?" he asked as they walked to the hotel.

"To be honest, there wasn't much new, but I did meet a man from Rotary who's looking for someone to work on a college exchange program in India."

"That should be right up your alley."

"It looks promising, if the timing works out. I go back to Africa in a week to finish up my Gates project."

They sat on stools at a counter and quickly got absorbed by the sushi makers' handiwork on the other side of the counter.

"Would you like some sake?" Jen asked.

"Why not? I'm celebrating."

"What's the occasion?"

"I'm retiring. Thirty-five years in a government bureaucracy does it for me."

"Oh, I'm happy for you, but sad for the world of development."

"I'm not leaving the field, just AID. I'm going to teach Development Studies part-time at American University in the fall."

"Fantastic."

"That's something you should consider. There's a real shortage of qualified academics."

They chatted about Nathan's other plans for retirement. He had a strong desire to travel for fun rather than work and, recently divorced, he was free to go wherever, whenever he wished. Jen suggested Africa. She could help set up a tour meeting his special interests.

He chuckled. "Be careful what you offer. I might take you up on that."

Walking home, she smiled. Mark and Nathan coming to tour Africa. She could well have gone into the travel business.

At home, a letter was waiting from Melinda Gates which, fearing for her grant, she opened nervously. In fact, it was a request for Jen to include Ruth, Melinda's South African assistant, on her visits in Uganda and Tanzania while Jen negotiated her five remaining deals. Ruth had never traveled outside South Africa, and Melinda wanted her to gain some field experience. Jen was delighted, hoping Ruth would report enthusiastically on her project and smooth the way for an ongoing grant. She arranged to meet Ruth in Arusha, Tanzania in two weeks' time.

Upon her return to Nairobi, Jen discovered Thabiri had been extremely conscientious about setting up meetings with village chiefs. With Ruth accompanying them, they visited two fairly advanced villages outside Arusha where the chiefs were eager for satellite dishes and internet connection. They wanted to offer tourists climbing Mount Kilimanjaro an add-on stay of a few days to experience rural Africa. They had to have an internet connection to advertise and communicate with clients.

Jen saw an opportunity to negotiate for girls' employment as well as education. When she added to the package deal not only girls' education but also their placement in agro-tourism jobs, surprisingly, the chiefs agreed. Apparently, a satellite dish was worth a lot.

∼

With the support of the Gates Foundation, Village Advantage was able to arrange a charter flight for Jen, Ruth and Thabiri, from Arusha to Kampala. Jen was grateful they could avoid the ten-hour bus ride she'd been planning. They flew over Serengeti National Park and Lake Victoria with breathtaking views of the lime-green terrain, the dramatic rift in the land, and a huge expanse of blue-gray water dotted with fishing boats.

In Uganda, Thabiri had set up visits to three villages, each in a different direction from Kampala. At each stop Jen insisted on meeting the village women before sitting down with the chief. In every case, the women chimed in that the village desperately needed a well because they lost a big portion of every day either going for water themselves or sending their children. When, in the meetings with the chiefs, the village leaders asked for satellite dishes, Jen came back with an offer of a well. When they insisted on dishes, she indicated her readiness to talk to other villages. As Thabiri had predicted, the chiefs, grumbling, came around.

The villages always invited the Village Advantage team for a meal. Normally, Jen would forgo the meal, but on these visits she accepted in order to give Ruth more of a flavor of village life. The meal was followed by drumming and dancing; the villagers were thrilled Ruth joined them in dancing.

On the flight back to Nairobi, Ruth, longing to be back in Africa, confessed she envied Jen's job.

"How would Melinda feel about that?" Jen asked.

"Fine. She can replace me easily. Everyone wants to work for Melinda."

"Well, let's see what happens. If Melinda decides to continue this project, I might be willing to have you take over."

~

And that's the way things worked out. Melinda was both pleased with the girls' education project and happy to have Ruth take over. At the same time, Jen was thrilled when Rotary offered her a consulting job in India. She agreed to start after her trip to Zanzibar with Mark and his daughter.

She made reservations for a two-bedroom cabin in Paje next to a gorgeous beach that was a center for kite-surfing. The hotel's chef served only fresh fish. Mark admitted he was more excited about Zanzibar than the safari.

And then it all fell apart.

Kate was bike-riding with her friends and, swerving away from a racing skate-boarder, fell on her arm and broke it in two places.

"Oh, poor Kate," Jen said on the phone. "She must be devastated."

"Actually, she loves the attention. I'm the one who's devastated. I even thought of leaving her with Marie and Yves, my au pairs, but she needs to stay home for two weeks and I've got to home school her."

"Well, we'll do it another time."

"Guess so." He hesitated then said, "I was able to cancel the safari for a small fee, but what about Zanzibar?"

"Well, since the cabin's non-refundable, I may go anyway. I have a friend at the Mission who might come with me."

"A male friend?"

She laughed. "You couldn't possibly be jealous."

"Of course, I am. Zanzibar sounded pretty romantic."

She cleared her throat. "My friend is a woman."

"That's a relief. And if she can't come, I'm paying for my half."

"Okay. Send Kate my love. Buy her a book about African animals for me."

∼

Jen's friend at the AID Mission was unable to join her. Jen considered going alone, but it would be much more fun with company. Just as she was ready to cancel, she got an email from Nathan saying he had loved his visit to Senegal and would soon be in East Africa. Should she invite Nathan? She knew she'd enjoy his company but was hesitant about jeopardizing a professional relationship with a personal invitation, especially if it involved staying in the same cabin. She emailed the hotel at Paje Beach to see if they had a free cabin and they were happy to provide one, although not on the beach. That was fine. She could take that cabin and was relieved they would cut the cost of the beach cabin to a single.

She dashed off an email to Nathan, explaining the Zanzibar situation and asking if he would like to join her. He replied in a day saying he had checked out flights and could come by way of Addis Ababa on the date she proposed. Jen was pleased. Nathan would be excellent company, and she definitely needed some time off before returning home. She suggested he take a taxi from the Zanzibar airport to Paje Beach where she'd meet him on March 27th.

∼

When, after a swim, Jen crossed the sand from the sea, she found Nathan reclining in a rattan chair on the veranda of his cabin, staring fixedly at the glittering turquoise water. Spotting her, he called out, "You didn't tell me one thing."

"What's that?"

"This is paradise. I can see why you wouldn't want to come alone, with no one to share it with."

She laughed. "Glad you get it. It'd be a shame for you to travel thousands of miles and be disappointed."

"Have a seat and tell me about our schedule."

She brushed sand off her feet, took the other chair, and outlined some possible excursions. They could visit traditional Stonetown; take a walk through the national park forest which had monkeys, tropical birds and butterflies; sail on a dhow to some outer islands.

"All of it," he exclaimed, "but my treat. You've been here before, and you're catering to me."

"It's no hardship, believe me. I propose we go to the forest tomorrow morning then come back here for the afternoon when the wind is up and the kite-surfers are out."

"Is that what I saw farther down the beach?"

"Yup. This is one of the world's centers for kite-surfing. It's gorgeous to watch, and you're welcome to try it but it's a lot—"

"Harder than it looks. This old guy is happy to watch."

"Me, too. Why don't I take a quick shower? Then we can have a drink at the bar, gaze at the sea, and have dinner."

∽

The evening went perfectly. Nathan had lots of tales to tell about West Africa. Jen filled him in on Arusha and Kampala. She told him about turning over the project so she could work for Rotary.

"Jen, I'm afraid the Mission has already offered your office to another nonprofit."

She chuckled. "Don't worry about it. The Gates Foundation has enough spare change to rent its own office space."

They took a walk on the beach after dinner. The tide was out and so were the stars. For Jen, it was lovely to be alone with an adult, especially Nathan, and not tugging along a seven-year old girl.

∼

The next day was full of excitement. In the morning, they caught sight of a large troop of howler monkeys swinging from tree to tree in the forest, totally oblivious to human visitors. In the afternoon a group of kite-surfers coursed through the water pulled by gorgeous, rainbow-colored kites. Jen took photo after photo of the rainbows for Maddie.

For dinner, loving the hotel restaurant, they took part a second time in a fresh fish barbecue washed down by a bottle of South African sauvignon blanc. It was a mellow night, primed for some personal conversation.

"If you'll excuse me, I've been wondering how a woman like you could be unattached, or maybe you're not," Nathan said.

Jen described her years with Dan in New York and her drawing away, given his obsession with work.

"Sounds a lot like my marriage. My wife was obsessed with money. She couldn't bear having me retire, give up a good federal salary, and travel 'like a gypsy' as she put it."

"After 35 years, she wanted you to keep working?"

"How else could we afford the house she craved in the Palisades?"

"Aha. I see why you split."

"I'm glad you get it. Some just don't understand."

They continued the pattern of the previous evening and took a stroll on the beach.

"Jen," he said softly, "I haven't had female companionship since my divorce." He stopped, looked out to sea then at her. "Would it be acceptable to hold your hand while we walk?"

She was touched by his diffidence, so different from Mark. She reached for his hand. "Much nicer to walk hand in hand."

When they eventually got back to the hotel, Jen squeezed his hand on his cabin steps. "Sleep well, and tomorrow, lots of lotion for the dhow. The sun will be intense."

"What about a snorkel and fins?"

"They have all that on the boat. But don't forget your camera."

"It's already in my beach bag. Sweet dreams."

"You, too. See you at 7 a.m. for coffee."

He grinned. "Another day in paradise."

∽

The day cruising on the dhow, the last day of touring Stonetown and catching kite-surfing again on the beach, in fact, their whole stay, was filled with laughter, interesting talk, and affection. Yet, they kept their warming feelings toward each other unspoken.

The next day, departure day, their flights left within an hour of each other, Jen to Nairobi, Nathan back to Addis. They planned to re-connect in a month in D.C. where Jen would have at least six weeks before taking off for India.

Nathan, picking up her carry-on bag, walked her to security. "I was wondering how I'd feel at the end of my African adventure, and now I know."

"Really? How?"

"Eager to see you again in Washington."

She put her hand in his. "It will be springtime – azaleas, rhododendron, wine in my garden."

"All those flowers in your garden?"

She laughed. "No way. It's small. Only a couple of pots of geraniums."

"I love geraniums." They were at the security gate. "I can't thank you enough for Zanzibar."

"My pleasure," she said. "And I mean it. I'm glad I had the nerve to email you."

"I am, too."

Chapter 24

Just before leaving Nairobi, Jen emailed Maddie to remind her she was coming home and was eager to see her dear buddy. She mentioned the trip to Zanzibar with Nathan, which was enough to propel Maddie from Connecticut to Washington for Jen's first weekend home. She was delighted Maddie was coming, but warned her there was no romance to analyze, just a rewarding friendship.

Jen arrived home on a Thursday; Maddie was arriving Friday afternoon. That gave Jen just enough time to make up the guest bed and stock her fridge and wine rack. She also bought eight geranium plants in pink, coral and white for the pots in her garden, smiling as she thought back to Nathan's comment that he loved geraniums. He'd be back in two weeks when the late April weather would be perfect for outdoor cocktail hours.

Maddie's cab pulled up, and she bounded out. Jen stood eagerly waiting on her front steps. They hugged as if they hadn't seen each other in years. Jen took Maddie to the tiny upstairs guest room and went to the one-person kitchen to open a bottle of white wine while Maddie washed up. They settled in the garden, bowls of nuts and olives on the round table between them.

"First," Maddie declared, "you've got to tell me about this Nathan guy."

Jen described how she'd met Nathan at USAID and had taken him for a sushi lunch. "That was all there was to it except I set him up with some contacts I had in Senegal."

"But you thought of him right away when Mark cancelled out on you."

"True." She sighed. "Zanzibar isn't the kind of place to be alone."

"So, tell me all about it."

Jen went through each day and, by the end, her pleasure with Nathan's company was evident.

"All good news," Maddie said. "And this time I can join you." She lifted her wine glass. "I, too, have a new friend."

"Heavens," Jen burst out. "I've been doing all the talking. Fill me in."

Maddie launched into a description of Patricia, a counselor at the University of Hartford whom she'd met at a lesbian bar. "She's beautiful, smart, and black."

"You only met her recently?"

"She's new on her campus, moved from L.A."

"Another world from Hartford."

"No kidding, no more city life for Patricia. But we plan to spend a lot of time in New York. Wish you still lived there."

"Well, you'll just have to come to D.C."

"As soon as we can."

They talked about the following day's schedule. Since Jen had to write a report for Gates, Maddie decided to spend the day at the National Gallery. They agreed to meet up for dinner at Café Central on Pennsylvania Avenue.

Before she went to bed, Jen checked her email – a welcome home message from Mark and an update on Ethiopia from Nathan, who closed on a tender note. "Each night, before I go to sleep, I imagine us walking on the beach in Paje under a blanket of stars."

～

Running late the next afternoon, Jen flagged a cab to get to Café Central on time. Just as the cab was crossing 12th St. on Pennsylvania Avenue, a car came blasting through the intersection at incredible speed and slammed into the mid-section of the taxi. The door of the back seat crumpled inward, crushing Jen. The taxi spun around and hit another car in the line of traffic.

Horns blared from every direction but, unconscious, Jen didn't hear them. A police car and an emergency fire truck arrived in minutes. She was pulled from the seat, placed onto a stretcher, and loaded onto the truck which rushed to GWU hospital.

The hospital put Jen in the ICU and prepared her for a head-to-toe examination. The emergency room support staff retrieved her cell phone from her purse but had no pass code to open it. A woman on the staff was dispatched to Jen's home a few blocks away with Jen's keys. When the staffer discovered Maddie's suitcase in the guest room with a luggage tag, she was able to find an email to Maddie on Jen's laptop. She was in the process of emailing her when Maddie burst in the townhouse door shouting loudly for Jen. The staffer did her best to calm Maddie and together they rushed back to the hospital.

By the time Maddie could see the ER doctor, a young Indian man with a short goatee, she learned Jen had regained consciousness but was not allowed visitors.

"Doctor Patel, I'm going crazy. What happened?" she cried.

"What is your relation to the patient?"

Maddie was frantic. "For God's sake, I'm her best friend."

"We need a member of the family."

"There is no close family – no parents, no husband, no partner. I'm the closest you can get."

"We'll have to verify that. What is her place of employment?"

"She's self-employed, a consultant. She works in Africa, just got back. Listen, you have to tell me what happened."

"A car slammed into her cab."

"Jesus. What about Jen?"

"Ms. Jacobs was injured by the cab door thrusting inward. Her hip was crushed. She'll need surgery once her condition is stabilized."

Maddie gripped the doctor's arm. "Stabilized? What else is wrong?"

The doctor stepped back. "Miss _____? What did you say your name is?"

"Johnson."

"Miss Johnson, we are checking her for a TBI."

"A what?"

"Traumatic brain injury."

"Oh, my God." She reached for the wall to steady herself.

"I don't want to upset you," the doctor said, stroking his beard. "Many TBIs are mild, with no lasting effect. Your friend's pupils dilated in bright light. That's a good sign. She'll have a full neurological exam tomorrow morning."

"I want to see her," Maddie demanded.

"I'm sorry. It's best for her to sleep now. She's sedated. You may be able to see her tomorrow afternoon."

"How long will she be here?"

"It all depends on what she needs in the way of surgery. We'll know much more in a day or so. I suggest you go home now and come back after noon tomorrow."

She took a deep breath, muttered, "Thank you," and turned to leave. As soon as she got back to Jen's, she sent out emails – one to Mark, one to Miriam at GWU, and, after only a minute's hesitation, one to Nathan.

She then wrote her dean at the honors program at Storrs and explained her need to take off a few days following the weekend.

∼

Maddie and Miriam met up at the hospital at noon on Sunday. They sought out Dr. Patel with no luck but were able to speak with an ICU nurse who indicated Maddie, while not a relative, had nonetheless been cleared as a visitor. She pushed the nurse for news. Jen seemed to have suffered only a modest brain injury that, most likely, would heal over time. She warned Maddie, however, that there were prescribed ways for visitors to interact with TBI patients and handed her a brochure. "These instructions are important," she said. "Please observe them."

"What about the surgery?" Maddie pressed.

"You'll have to talk to Dr. Patel about that."

"Where is he?"

"I'll let him know you're here."

Maddie sat down in a chair next to Miriam, and they studied the brochure. Visitors were instructed never to argue or disagree with a TBI patient, never to correct the patient's views of reality. The only way to interact with a TBI patient was to go along.

"God." Maddie groaned. "It makes her sound like a nut case."

"Read the last bit," Miriam urged. "In the case of mild TBIs, 95 percent recover fully. It's just a question of time."

"How much time?"

"Doesn't say."

Spotting Dr. Patel down the hall, Maddie sped toward him. He guided her back to the chairs, assuring her and Miriam he'd update them as fully as he could. "Your friend's pelvis was crushed by the door of the cab. We need to insert a metal pelvis to replace the crushed bone. There is one expert in town for designing a new pelvis. He's at Georgetown University Hospital."

"Well, let's move her there," Maddie said.

"Actually, Dr. Amit will be here in an hour to exam Ms. Jacobs. Once he produces a metal replacement, we'll schedule surgery to insert it."

"Here?"

"Yes. It's best not to move her."

"Can I see her now?"

"We're keeping her sedated for the pain. Agitation, excitement would not be good for her."

Maddie shook her head. "This evening?"

"Come back to the ICU after 6 p.m."

Maddie hugged Miriam as they parted then trudged back to Jen's. There was a message on her phone to call Mark at 2 p.m., 11 a.m. California time. She fixed herself a sandwich and took it to the garden. What should she tell Mark, especially since she hadn't yet seen Jen? Even more, she wondered what to tell him about coming to visit.

She need not have worried about Mark's visit. He took care of that on his own. After she gave him the details on the TBI and pelvic surgery, he made clear he was unable to travel until he got his kids settled with the new au pair couple.

"How long will that be?" Maddie asked.

"I don't know, probably a week or ten days."

"I need to get back to work in a week or ten days. It would be great if you could come earlier."

"I can't leave the kids."

"What about your wife?"

"She'll only come for a couple of days."

Maddie felt irritated. "Mark, we're talking about Jen, your long-term friend. She needs you now."

"I'm doing the best I can. Let me know as soon as she's out of surgery so I can send flowers."

"Right."

∽

Back at the hospital by 6 p.m., Maddie waited an hour to see Dr. Patel. He told her cheerfully that Dr. Amit had worked in his lab all Sunday fashioning a metal pelvis and would be inserting it the next day.

"Thank goodness. What kind if name is Amit?"

"Israeli. He knows what he's doing."

Maddie felt slightly better. "Does Jen know she's having surgery?"

"Yes, but not the details. It's better not to say anything about her pelvis."

"So, can I see her now?"

He nodded. "Five minutes, no more. A nurse will take you in. Don't try to converse. Just let her know you're here."

The nurse came by and took Maddie by the arm. "Don't ask her any questions. Just reassure her you're standing by."

While Maddie had been prepared Jen would be hooked up to a number of monitors, she hadn't been warned about the head and body brace. Jen's eyes were shut but when Maddie spoke her name, they fluttered open.

"I'm here, my love," Maddie said. "And I'll be here for your operation and after. You are not alone." She turned to the nurse. "Can I kiss her?"

"You can touch her hand."

She gently held Jen's fingers. "I love you, sweetheart. We all do. We'll be here to hug right after the operation."

The nurse pulled Maddie's arm away and led her out of the unit.

Chapter 25

Exhausted by the time she got back to Jen's, Maddie quickly scanned her email, had a brief chat with Patricia in Hartford, and fell into bed. She slept soundly and woke, completely disoriented by the ringing doorbell. She yelled out, "Coming," and threw on a robe.

At the door, a man with curly gray hair, a deep tan, and holding a large backpack upright, said, "You must be Jen's friend, Maddie. Thank you for your email."

Startled, she said, "Nathan? Aren't you supposed be in Africa?"

"When I got your message, I got on the first plane I could. How is she?"

"Wow. Come in. I'll catch you up. She has surgery this afternoon. Come in, come in. I've got coffee."

Nathan left his backpack in the hall. Maddie pulled a towel out of the cabinet under the stairs and sent him upstairs to wash up. When he came back down, she told him she was making bacon and eggs.

"There's nothing we can do for Jen today," she said. "She's in pre-op this morning and her operation is at three. English muffin?"

"Thank you. The food on the plane was hardly appetizing."

She handed him full plates to take to the garden while she brought out the coffee pot and two mugs. "Dig in and I'll tell you all I know."

She covered the accident, the TBI and crushed pelvis, the pelvic expert from Georgetown University hospital. "I have no idea how long she'll be in the hospital, but I'm sure glad you're here. I have to leave in a few days."

"No problem. Does Jen have anyone else in D.C.? Family, friends?"

"No family, one good friend, Miriam from GWU. Maybe other friends, but I haven't met them." She wasn't going to say a word about Mark. "I'm her closest friend. We got to know each a few years ago."

"She told me about you."

"And she told me a little about you. Where do you live?"

"I've got an apartment on Capitol Hill, but it's rented out for another ten days. I'll find a place to stay."

"Don't be silly. Stay here. Jen won't be out of the hospital for some time."

"I can't stay here, but thank you."

Maddie crossed her arms and glared. "You're staying here. In Jen's bedroom. I'd give you the guest room, but the bed barely fits me."

She started to clear the plates then said, "Can you help with this? I'm going upstairs to change the bed. You must need sleep, and we don't have to be at the hospital until three."

∼

When Maddie and Nathan, perspiring from the humidity, got to the hospital at 3 p.m., they were directed to a waiting room outside the surgical unit. Maddie asked how long the operation would take, but no one answered directly.

"I hate hospitals," she muttered.

"Until you have an accident," Nathan responded

"Don't be so reasonable."

"I feel impatient too, but let them take the time they need to do it right."

It turned out to be a two-hour operation. When Dr. Patel came out to see them, he was all smiles. "It went well. Your friend has a new pelvis and should heal completely."

"Thank goodness," Maddie said, "and thank you."

"Thank Dr. Amit. He made quite a piece of hardware, but Ms. Jacobs should never know it's there."

"How long will she be in here?"

"That mostly depends on her TBI."

"Can you give us a ballpark figure?" She looked at Nathan then back at the doctor. "This is Jen's friend, Nathan Perlstein."

"Hello. Look, this is a very rough guess. She'll need a lot of rehab, so I'd say a month."

"Whew!"

Nathan took her arm. "Don't worry, Maddie. I'll be here." He turned to the doctor. "When can we see Ms. Jacobs?"

"Come back tomorrow evening. For now, go home and rest."

They gathered their things. On the way out, Maddie suggested they stop by Trader Joe's to pick up some dinner. They loaded up on enough ribs and barbecued chicken to last a few days.

As they walked in the front door, Maddie announced she needed a drink. She opened one of the red wines they'd picked up and they took their glasses of wine to the living room couch.

"Here's to Jen's recovery," she said. "And to good friends."

"You win the prize for that," Nathan said.

"I was talking about you. I know you two enjoyed your time in Zanzibar, but I still can't believe you ended your Africa trip to get here."

He smiled. "There's always travel. There's only one Jen."

On the verge of tears, Maddie compared his response to Mark's unwillingness to get on a plane until he had his home life organized. A world of difference. "Nathan, how do you think Jen's gonna feel about you coming home?"

"Not sure. Frankly, I'm not even sure she'll be able to think that coherently for a while. I just hope she's glad to see me."

"I have no doubt about that."

∼

The next day, during the time Jen was in post-op, Maddie and Nathan did chores around the house, including a wash of Nathan's travel clothes. Maddie put together a small suitcase for Jen with nightclothes, shampoo, skin creams and light cosmetics. Nathan pulled together some reading and television schedules. By 6 p.m., they were ready for Jen; privately, they wondered what kind of shape she'd be in.

Maddie had given Nathan the brochure on TBIs. "We've got to remember to go along with whatever she says. Conflict is the worst thing for her."

"Don't worry. I'll be pleased if she takes in the fact that we're there for her."

Arriving at the hospital, they were relieved to learn Jen had just been moved from the ICU to a private room. They were told to come back in an hour and they went to the hospital cafeteria for a bite.

∼

The floor nurse insisted on only one visitor at a time and limited to a five-minute visit. Maddie took the first turn and was delighted to find Jen in a slightly upraised bed, her lower half, in bandages, held in place by straps hanging from an overhead device.

"Jen, my love, it's Maddie."

Jen opened her eyes, a hint of a smile on her face. "Hi, Ma—" She struggled with the name.

"Sweetie, they won't let me kiss you, but imagine my arms around you in a long hug. They put you back together and we're gonna get you out of the hospital and back home soon."

She tried to smile.

"Best of all, I have a wonderful surprise. A man you care about has come to visit."

Her eyes opened wider, not apparently in pleasure. "No Mark."

Maddie was taken aback. "No, not Mark. It's Nathan. He's back from Africa. Do you want to see Nathan?"

She nodded.

"Good. As soon as I leave, I'll send him in."

Jen closed her eyes.

"Sweetie, I brought some things from home." Maddie realized Jen was too groggy. "Never mind. Tomorrow. I love you, my dear friend."

No response. Maddie went out to the hall and warned Nathan. "She's pretty out of it, but she'll be glad to see your face."

He signaled to the nurse who led him into the room. "Five minutes tops."

"Jen, it's Nathan."

Her eyes opened and this time, a real smile. "Na…Zan…"

"Yup. We last saw each other at the Zanzibar Airport. I've missed you."

She stared.

"We'll see each other a lot as you heal from your surgery."

"Okay."

Her eyes closed again and the nurse beckoned toward the door. "Enough excitement for tonight. Come back tomorrow. Visiting hours."

Chapter 26

The next day Nathan and Maddie were at the hospital at ten a.m., the start of visiting hours. Again, the nurse would only allow one visitor in at a time and for only a few minutes. To Maddie, Jen seemed no different from the day before – groggy, passive, barely able to keep her eyes open. According to Nathan, she perked up a little during his visit. She said, "Africa, trip, beach, stars." He decided to come back in the evening with his photos of Zanzibar and a picture book on African game.

Happily, when they returned at six p.m., Jen was more alert. During Maddie's time, Jen pointed to her hair and said, "Dirty." Maddie asked the nurse about a hair wash and was told "in a few days."

On the table at the foot of Jen's bed stood a huge arrangement of red roses, white daisies and baby's breath. Maddie was sure they were from Mark and said, "Lovely flowers." Jen pointed to the corner of the room and said, "There."

Maddie picked up the vase and carried it to the table by the window. "Better?"

Jen nodded.

During Nathan's time, Jen smiled broadly, especially when he presented her with a pot of pink geraniums tied up with a white bow. As they looked at the photos on his phone, she reached for the phone and held it to her chest.

Next, he brought out the photo book of African game. It was too heavy for her to hold up but she said, "Read." Nathan held up shots of different animals and read the text underneath until Jen drifted off to sleep.

∽

"So, what do you think?" Maddie asked Nathan as they left the hospital.

"She's improving but has a long way to go."

She frowned. "I know, and I have to leave tomorrow afternoon."

"How do you get to Storrs?"

"I fly to Hartford. My girlfriend will pick me up."

"I'll miss you, but, don't worry about it, Jen. I'll be there every day."

"And you'll call or email me every night with a report?"

"You bet." He looked off into the distance. "Should I expect any other visitors? Like the person who sent the roses?"

"That's a long story." They were approaching Jen's townhouse. "How about we do that over a glass of wine?"

The evening remained comfortably warm and they sat out in the garden with a chicken salad Maddie put together and a bottle of white wine. She wasn't sure what to say about Jen's relationship with Mark. She didn't want Nathan to think of them as partners, but she needed to acknowledge they were long-standing and close friends despite Mark's marriage, children, and move to California. She began with the years at CUNY, moved on to Mark's move to Stanford, divorce, and custody of the children.

"If you don't mind me saying this," Nathan commented, "they must be more than just friends."

Maddie hesitated. "Part of the relationship was physical but they were – oh, how do I put this? – they were conjugal very infrequently."

Nathan pursed his lips. "If red roses are any indication, he still feels romantic."

"Possibly, but Jen? Well, you'd have to ask her. I'd say she appreciates the pink geranium far more than the roses."

There was a long pause in the conversation. Finally, Maddie said, "I expect Mark will come to see Jen. I don't know when."

"I'm surprised he hasn't come already."

"He needed to work out arrangements for his kids." Leaving it at that, she took their plates to the kitchen.

∽

The next morning, after Maddie had packed her bag, she proposed to Nathan that she go for the morning visit with Jen and he come in the evening.

"Girl talk," he said with a grin.

"Something like that. I feel bad about leaving. I want Jen to know I'll be back soon. Also, I'm meeting Miriam at the hospital, and I think they only allow two visitors."

Smiling, he gave a thumb's-up. "As I said, girl talk. Please give Miriam my phone number."

"She already has it."

∽

Maddie found Miriam in the waiting area of the hospital's third floor and gave her a hug. She reminded her about the TBI rules and sent her in first. When it was her turn, Maddie was amazed to find Jen fully alert and able to speak complete sentences.

"You're doing so well, my friend," Maddie said. "I don't feel so bad about leaving."

"Come back soon."

"I'll be back in a week."

Jen's face lit up with a full smile. "Come back with your friend."

"I just might do that." She looked toward the roses by the window. "Speaking of friends, Mark has been texting me about coming to visit."

"Why?"

"To see you, of course."

"He can call."

"Sweetie, they don't want you to have phone service yet."

Jen looked toward the phone. "Why?"

"They want you to rest. Soon, I'm sure."

"Okay." She began to fade, her eyes fluttering closed.

Maddie got up and kissed her forehead. "A goodbye kiss until my next visit."

Jen smiled, half-asleep.

When she came out to the waiting area, Maddie was surprised to see Nathan in place of Miriam.

"How is she?" he asked.

"Much better today. We had a conversation. I feel more relaxed about leaving." She looked him in the eye. "Glad to see you. but you're not supposed to be here now. Where's Miriam?"

"She had to go. She'll be back tomorrow. I brought your suitcase so we could have a more leisurely goodbye."

"Good. This gives us a few more minutes. Listen, Jen was upset she has no phone service. Apparently, they do that with TBI cases because they sometimes make wacky calls."

"Got that."

"She said she was willing to talk to Mark but wasn't eager to see him. I hate to leave you in the middle of all this. I'll call Mark and suggest he come when I'm here. Like next weekend. I hope Jen is ready to handle the stress of him visiting by then."

"Good idea for you to be here." He gave her a hug. "Jen and I are going to have a good week. By the time you get back, she'll be reading the *Washington Post.*"

"Ha! I'd settle for the tv schedule." She kissed his cheek. "Nathan, it has been a gift to have you here."

He picked up her suitcase. "Let me put you in a cab."

"No way. I'm calling Uber."

∽

The week to follow was one of steady progress for Jen. The doctors wanted her to move her legs but not put weight on her hip. They fixed her up with crutches to get to the bathroom. Rosa, a new, extremely cheerful Filipina nurse, who worked the morning shift, was happy to wash Jen's hair in the bathroom. She also brought in a variety of games, mostly children's board games, but also a few simple word games Jen was ready for.

"One of these days I'm gonna beat you at Scrabble," she told Nathan. "'Til then, these are supposed to get my brain working again."

He was amazed at how well she understood her condition. Two neurologists had started making calls to test her cognitive skills. She had no problem naming the month of the year or Clinton as President, but was at a loss when it came to the day of the week. She had Nathan write a small calendar on a post-it which she stuck to her nightstand. As soon as she saw the neurologists at her doorway, she checked the calendar in order to answer the day of the week correctly.

Every other day she was put in a wheelchair and taken downstairs for occupational therapy. She told Nathan she felt like an idiot putting round pegs in round holes.

"Think of it as a way to get out of your room and check out the rest of the hospital."

"They could at least take me to the cafeteria for some decent food."

"You are getting a bit thin. What can I bring you?"

"Ice cream and chocolate."

"What kind?"

"Popsicles, chocolate-covered, and Nestle's Crunch."

"Okay. I'll sneak them in at night, but you'll have to eat the Popsicle right away before it melts."

"No problem."

~

During his evening visits, Nathan read to Jen, often books like *Out of Africa* or novels by new African writers. She usually fell asleep in half an hour, but always remembered the next morning to thank him for reading.

~

Late Wednesday evening during their nightly call, Nathan and Maddie discussed Mark's visit. He'd made reservations for Friday in order to see Jen on Saturday and Sunday. Jen was open to a visit, she'd said, but she didn't want Mark at her house. That was for Nathan. And she wanted to be sure Maddie would be outside in the hall

"Why does she want you in the hall?" he asked.

"She's nervous." She cleared her throat. "Mark seems to want more than she's prepared to give."

"Well, Maddie to the rescue."

"I hope it doesn't come to that."

~

Maddie got back to D.C. late Friday night, said a quick hello to Nathan, and crashed in the guest room.

On Saturday, Mark showed up promptly at ten, bearing a dozen long-stemmed roses, yellow this time. Maddie insisted he read the TBI brochure.

He glanced at it, looked up and said, "How long have I got?"

"Half an hour now, and you can come back at six."

"Fine." He pushed open the door of the room and found Jen dozing but she opened her eyes when she heard his voice.

He handed Rosa the flowers and kissed Jen's head. "How are you doing?"

"Okay. Thanks for the flowers."

He pointed to the crutches. "Are you allowed to walk?"

"To the bathroom. They want me to keep weight off my hip."

"Can you leave the room?"

"Only for therapy. In a wheelchair. Why all the questions?"

"Well, I had an idea. I thought you might like to recuperate in California. It's not hot like here, no humidity."

"You've got enough on your hands."

"Not really. The twins are in pre-K, and Kate is consumed by ballet and swimming. She goes to ballet class every morning and the pool every afternoon. The au pair couple chauffeurs them around."

"Sounds good." She changed the subject. "Where are you staying?"

"Remember when I gave the talk at Georgetown? The Tabard Inn?"

She nodded her head.

"You remember. Excellent. So, I'm staying with the professor who invited me. I'm going to speak to his summer seminar on Monday."

"Good."

"Jen, are you sure you don't want to come to Palo Alto?"

She nodded.

"Is there a reason?"

"My doctor is here. My friends are here." She pressed the buzzer for the nurse.

Mark got the message. "Can I come back at six?"

"Uh-huh." She closed her eyes.

Back in the waiting room, Maddie asked Mark, "How'd it go?"

"Honestly, I don't know. I invited her to California and she seemed quite negative."

"She's comfortable here, Mark. This is home."

"She'd have three people to take care of her. Me and the au pair couple."

"And three little kids running around. Mark, she needs rest. She should be going home in a couple of weeks."

He looked incredulous. "To a house where she has to climb stairs to use the bathroom."

"We'll work something out. Good to see you."

"I'll be back at six." He turned and left.

Chapter 27

Maddie went in to see Jen a few minutes after Mark's visit. Jen's eyes were closed. Maddie sat down quietly to wait.

Eyes still closed, Jen mumbled, "No California."

"Got you, sweetie. Have a good sleep." Maddie left and made her way back to Jen's house.

After hearing about Mark's visit, Nathan said angrily, "What's wrong with the guy?"

"Apparently, Jen's got to be more explicit, but I'm worried that could bring on conflict, which would not be good for her."

"Maddie, you've got to be Jen's spokesperson."

She snorted. "With Mark? That would really bring on conflict."

They sat quietly for a moment then Nathan said, "You could send him an email."

She searched his face. "No one-on-one? Yeah. Will you help?"

"Get a pad."

They worked in the living room. After numerous corrections and rephrasings, they came up with a draft they could live with.

Dear Mark:

I'm taking the liberty of speaking for Jen, who has expressed these feelings to me at different times but is not capable right now of speaking for herself. She greatly values your friendship, has since you met six years ago. Yet, when you proposed being partners, living together in California, she knew that would not work for her. She wants you to have a partner, someone with whom you join fully in the life you've chosen. She wants you to be with someone who thrives on domesticity, family life, children. We both know Jen well. She pretty much gets what she wants. If she wanted domesticity and family, she'd have it by now.

I know Jen wants to maintain your friendship. I know she wishes the best for you. So do I.

Fondly, Maddie

Nathan smiled. "It's a fine, balanced letter. Do you think we should show it to Jen?"

"Heavens no. I'm afraid of upsetting her." She got up from the couch, reached for the ceiling in a long stretch. "Let's send it and see what he says."

"You're a good friend, Maddie."

"I hope Jen agrees."

Late in the afternoon, Mark texted Maddie. "Will be at hospital at six."

She exploded. "Not a word about my email. What the hell does that mean?"

"His pride is hurt. He's looking for a graceful exit."

"Graceful? Hard to believe."

He looked at his watch. "Let's go back to the hospital. We'll find out soon enough."

"He might not like having you there."

"Agreed. I'll sit apart, away from you unless needed."

"Thanks."

~

When Mark, carrying a small package in a manila envelope, showed up at the hospital waiting room, his manner was distinctly cold. Maddie looked back at Nathan in the last row of chairs to reassure herself then said, "Hello, Mark. Six o'clock on the nose."

"Can I go in?"

"Sure. As a gentle reminder, please remember the TBI rules. She needs to stay calm."

"Relax." He turned and headed toward Jen's room.

"Hi," she said when he came in. She clicked off the tv. "As usual, all the news is bad."

He placed his package on the nightstand, sat on the edge of the bed. "That's how they keep their customers happy. How was your day?"

"Fascinating," she said sarcastically.

He reached in his shirt pocket and withdrew a sheet of paper. "This is an email I received from Maddie. She says she's writing on your behalf. Do you know anything about this?"

"No."

"I thought not." He passed her the paper. "Take a look."

She read through it slowly, lay her head back on the pillow, stared at the ceiling.

"Is she accurately reflecting your views?"

Jen straightened up, picked up the email message and read through it again. "Pretty much. You know how much I care for you and I do wish you'd find a partner who wants the same things you do."

"That's not you?"

She looked into his eyes. "No, not me."

"Well, that pretty much settles things. I'm glad I heard it from you and not just Maddie."

"Me, too."

He walked to the window, stood by his roses and stared out silently for a moment. Then he turned, picked up the manila envelope and placed it beside her on the bed. "For you."

"Another gift? You've given me so many already."

"This one's special."

She opened the envelope, pulled out something soft wrapped in tissue paper, and looked at him. "Lingerie?"

"Not exactly."

Tearing off the tissue paper, she found a pale yellow tee shirt with large print across the front declaring "FRIEND" with "fnfe" underneath. "Wow! Terrific!"

"I have a matching shirt. And I know you're going to ask what 'fnfe' means."

"So?"

"Well, I'm not going to tell you. When you figure it out, our friendship will be bonded."

"It already is."

"Bonded permanently."

She smiled. "Okay. I'll work on it."

He sat down again on the bed, took her hand in his. "I'm not sure when I'll see you again, but we have the phone and email."

"I'm not sure they'll let me use either 'til I get out of here."

"Any idea when?"

Laughing, she said, "I've got all the round pegs in the round holes, so I hope soon."

He leaned over and kissed her head. "Call me as soon as you can."

"You know I will. Thanks for coming and 'fnfe,' whatever that means."

He kissed her again and left.

He passed Maddie as he strode toward the waiting room exit. "Sent you an email with my plans." No goodbye. Obviously he was hurting.

Maddie beckoned to Nathan. "Let's go in together."

Jen sat, looking smug, arms across her chest. "That was a good message you wrote. Co-authorship?"

Nathan winked. Maddie shrugged.

Jen held up the tee shirt. "Well, we're staying friends, and we're both free to move on."

Chapter 28

It was coming up on a month since Jen had been hospitalized. She was feeling incredibly restless. That morning, she'd been through her regular routine of washing up, breakfast, watching *Morning Joe* on MSNBC. It was still an hour until Nathan would show up for visiting hours.

She was reaching for a Nadine Gordimer novel on her nightstand when Dr. Patel poked his head in from the hall. "Come in, come in," she cried. "I hope you're here with good news."

"I believe so, but first let me check your scar."

"There are two of them. No more bikinis." She rolled onto her right side and lifted her hospital gown. The doctor concluded she was healing nicely. She covered up, pushed back up to a sitting position and demanded the good news.

He announced she'd be ready to go home in a couple of days. She cheered. The therapists had all cleared her, even though the neurologists reported she cheated on one of their questions.

"Come on. Only on the day of the week. And today's Wednesday," she said, puffed up with pride. "So, when can I leave?"

He rubbed his hand over his goatee. "As soon as your house is ready."

"It is ready. My friend Nathan has been staying there and taking good care of it."

"Yes, we've spoken with him. Unfortunately, there are a couple of problems."

"Like what?"

"Your townhouse is two floors with the bedroom and bathroom upstairs. We don't want you climbing stairs for at least a month. We also want you to remain in bed for another thirty days, in a hospital bed. Your pelvis needs support. If you take any steps, do so only with a cane."

Jen was speechless. She'd been expecting to walk out.

"Fortunately, your friend has some ideas. You two can discuss them when he arrives." The doctor turned to leave. "I'll be back tomorrow."

She felt frantic. She had to get out of the hospital. But how? She couldn't mooch off a friend for a whole month. She could hardly afford a hotel room for that time. Maybe an Air BnB. She needed her iPad to do a search, was again furious the hospital wouldn't provide internet.

Nathan knocked then let himself in. "So, you got the good news?"

She frowned. "Good? They'll let me out, but they won't let me go home."

"Don't jump to conclusions." He presented his plan to install Jen on the first floor with a rented hospital bed and portable toilet. She could put her living room couch in storage or move it to Nathan's apartment.

"Do you have room?"

"Plenty. My ex-wife kept all the furniture. I could use a couch, even temporarily." He looked uncomfortable then said, "We could also switch apartments. You could stay at my place and I could stay at yours."

"Nathan, that's sweet, but even if I have to wash up in the kitchen, I really want to go home."

"I thought you'd say that. I've already checked the prices for the bed and toilet. Your insurance will cover both."

"Gosh, great. When can we move the couch?"

"Tomorrow, if you agree to put it in my place."

"Why not? Oh, Nathan, I'm going home. You're making it possible. Thank you, thank you, thank you."

Early Thursday morning, Nathan greeted two student movers who took Jen's couch to his apartment. He stopped in briefly at the hospital then rushed back to Jen's house for the delivery of the bed and toilet.

Friday morning, she said a warm goodbye to Rosa and was taken by wheelchair to an ambulance. Embarrassed to arrive home in an ambulance, she nonetheless cheered when her neighbors showed up with casseroles and snacks. She asked Nathan to stay the night and help her get settled. His first move was to set up a stand over the hospital bed for meals and her laptop.

At six p.m. Nathan brought out a bottle of champagne which Jen insisted they drink in the garden, although stepping over the threshold of the French doors and down into the patio was definitely challenging. She needed his help. "Damn. By the time I can walk properly, it will be September."

"Patience, Jen. Autumn is perfect in this town for strolls through the neighborhood and around the Mall."

Pouting, she said, "With a cane."

"Better than crutches."

"Sorry. I'm being a brat. Open the champagne. Let's celebrate."

They clinked their flutes at the garden table, surrounded by geraniums. "You kept this so beautiful," she said.

"Don't worry. I'll be back from time to time to water."

"More often than that, please."

"Well, you have Maddie and her girlfriend coming tomorrow."

"They want to see *you*."

"Hey, you don't need an old coot like me around."

"Nathan, I may not *need* you, but I *want* you around. Please don't disappear on me."

He smiled but said nothing as he filled their glasses.

∽

The next day, Saturday, Nathan slipped out at noon after he'd made Jen a sandwich for lunch. She was alone, no nurses, no visitors, for the first time in weeks. It felt odd but wouldn't last long since Maddie and Patricia were arriving in time for dinner.

She lay back and reflected on the lows and highs of the last few weeks. The lows – dealing with Mark; putting round pegs in round holes; depending on crutches to limp to the bathroom. The highs – getting her first shampoo; hearing of her release from the hospital; Nathan. Nathan every morning and evening. She was needy and he was there.

The time with Nathan, even the anticipation of his visits, had made her hospital stay more than tolerable. Actually, at many times, pleasant. Nathan was the kind of partner she'd always wanted. He treated her as an equal, even when she had to lean on him. They were peers, each able to provide for the other. That made her exceedingly happy.

She reached for the button to raise up her bed. She might as well read now she had the chance. She had just started a nonfiction account of the Gates family sent by Melinda. If Melinda approved it, it would doubtless be positive and, she suspected, accurate. Reading, watching MSNBC and CNN, taking her usual afternoon nap took her to five p.m. Having had some alone time, she was more than ready for visitors.

Maddie and Patricia, who'd come by train from Hartford, showed up at six p.m. They'd stopped off for Thai take-out and Jen's small living room filled with the aromas of curry and musky spices.

Kissing Maddie, Jen said, "The upstairs is all yours. You can sleep together or separately, but if you want to watch tv, you've got to come down here."

"What I want is pot stickers and white wine in your garden," Maddie declared. "Can you maneuver out there?"

"I need a small assist."

Once they got settled around the garden table, Patricia asked Jen, "Are you in any pain?"

"Nope. They took me off painkillers a week ago. My main problem is boredom."

"This poor girl," Maddie said sarcastically. "She has a lovely man who waits on her hand and foot and she's complaining."

"Excuse me," Jen retorted, looking around. "I don't see any men."

"And when did he leave?"

"Noon."

They all burst out laughing.

Maddie popped a wonton in her mouth. "We're gonna do something special for Nathan. We're cooking him dinner tomorrow night and sending him home with a big bag of leftovers."

"He seems to think this visit is just for girls."

"That's ridiculous. I'm calling him right now."

She went inside for her phone, got Nathan on the line and instructed him to show up at seven for dinner. "No equivocating. It's my Caribbean jambalaya. You can bring wine if you like. White and cold."

Once she'd hung up, she turned to Jen. "Can we talk about Nathan?"

Jen wasn't surprised. She'd been expecting Maddie to go directly at it. "If you're asking about a hot relationship, there isn't one. Only a deep friendship."

"Isn't one yet. When is this friendship going to turn to love?"

"I knew you'd ask. Honestly, I'm ready to try, but something is holding him back."

"Maybe it's you," Maddie said. "Maybe he's afraid of falling in love with a sick woman."

"I'm not sick," Jen retorted. "I'm healing. Anyway, he doesn't have to commit to anything. He could just say something romantic."

Maddie turned to Patricia. "Let's ask the counselor. What do you think?"

Patricia clasped her hands in her lap. "This is tough. Nathan is a big boy, but he's recently been through a divorce. You need to go slowly, gently."

"But she could make clear her interest," Maddie said.

"Yes, but very gently."

∽

Sunday morning, Maddie and Patricia walked to Whole Foods to pick up the shrimp, sausage and spices for the jambalaya. The three women spent the afternoon watching old films on tv – Fred Astaire and Ginger Rogers, Humphrey Bogart and Lauren Bacall.

"Oh, to have love stories like those again," Maddie said.

"Strange words from a lesbian," Jen observed.

Patricia jumped in. "Romance is romance. Period."

Dinner with Nathan turned out to be great fun. Over several bottles of wine, they got him to open up about his early life. Jen learned a lot she'd never known and was reminded of other stories he'd shared with her in Africa. He'd gotten fascinated by developing countries after working as a military adviser in Vietnam during the war. He'd married a woman, who'd made a lovely home, but was more committed to her career than children. He'd buried himself in work most his life, gotten divorced when his wife made clear she had no interest in exploring the world with him once he retired.

Jen felt sad Nathan's life had been unfulfilling on the personal level. Yet, what about hers? Except for Mark, her life had also been all work, fulfilling work but still work.

Once Nathan had left and her friends had gone up to bed, Jen reflected on Nathan's reserve. Was it his recent divorce? Was it her accident? Was it Mark? She was puzzled but needed to get to the bottom of it, gently, of course, ever so gently.

Monday morning, as Maddie and Patricia finished an early breakfast with Jen before their train, Maddie said, "Anyone want to re-hash last night?"

"I had a great time," Patricia said, "but after all that wine, I hardly remember a thing."

"You don't remember describing the two lesbian cruises you took?" Maddie joked.

"You're jealous you weren't there."

"I don't like cruises."

"Too bad, 'cause I just put down a deposit for a Virgin Islands cruise at Christmas."

"For us?" she screeched. "The Caribbean at Christmas?"

"Yeah, but since you don't like cruises..."

"Maybe I should try one more time."

Jen chuckled. "You two are quite a pair."

Once they'd left their bags at the front door, Maddie and Patricia perched on either side of Jen's bed to say goodbye. Maddie took Jen's hand. "This bed will be gone the next time I see you."

"Please God."

Patricia smoothed out the sheet. "May I say one more serious thing?"

"Yes, counselor."

"I got the feeling last night that Nathan is in love with you but something is blocking him."

"Me, too." Maddie squeezed Jen's hand. "Be brave, girl. Find out what it is."

Jen sighed. "I'll give it a try."

"Keep us posted." Maddie and Patricia each kissed a cheek and took off.

Chapter 29

Jen heard the mail drop through the slot in her front door to the hall floor. She usually left it there for Nathan to bring in when he came for dinner, but he hadn't called and she wasn't sure he was coming. Feeling bored and restless, she slid her legs over the side of the bed and reached for her cane. She wasn't supposed to bend over to pick up anything but she managed to hobble to the front door and with her cane push some envelopes and a *New Yorker* down the hall toward her bed. Once back on the bed, she could reach the floor for her mail.

Under the bills and solicitations was a letter from Rotary. She opened it anxiously. She had requested a nine-month delay for the start of her work in India, and they had taken several weeks to reply. Their response was devastating. They were extremely anxious to start the college exchange program and had decided to hire another consultant. They would keep her in mind for future projects.

She couldn't really blame them – nine months was a long time to wait – but now she had nothing to look forward to and would have to look for other projects from a hospital bed. That was not the way to find work in her field. It was all about networking, making calls on nonprofits to explore what they were doing and how she might fit into the picture.

Her phone dinged and she found a text from Nathan saying he'd be by around six with groceries and something for dinner. He'd stay if she wanted company or leave if, after her weekend visitors, she needed time alone. She didn't know what she wanted except to get back on her feet, literally and figuratively. She turned off her lamp and pulled the sheet up. She'd try napping. She'd gotten up so early a nap might improve her mood.

Sleep never came. She kept dwelling on her empty life – no work, no love life, no escape. The only thing she had to look forward to each day was a visit from Nathan, and she wondered how long that would last. Once she was mobile again, he might drop out of her life. Too depressing to think about. She clicked on the news for a distraction, found herself, like a zombie, staring at the screen without taking anything in.

Just as the news program was ending, Nathan bustled in with grocery bags and made his way to the kitchen. "I got salmon for dinner," he called out.

No response from Jen.

"Did you hear me?" he stored a few items in the fridge.

"Yup. Fine."

He strode into the living room, looking sporty in a light blue alligator shirt, took one look at her, and said, "What's wrong?"

She held out the letter from Rotary as a tear rolled down her cheek. "No job, no way to get one. In this town, they don't hire cripples."

He pulled the chair up next to her. "Jen, I understand you're disappointed, but there are still ways to find work. Okay, for now, you need a desk job, but there are plenty of those."

She shrugged. "I've got no idea how to get started."

"The same way everyone else does, with a reference."

"From you?"

"Sure, I'll write one, but one from Seattle would go a lot further."

Her eyebrows wrinkled. "Ask Melinda?"

"Why not? Call her now. It's only 3:30 p.m. on the West Coast."

"It's a beginning, I guess." She studied his face, smiled slowly. "You are always here for me."

While Nathan cut up broccoli, made a salad and put the salmon in a broiling pan, Jen thought about her call to Melinda. They hadn't been in touch since a few days after her accident when Melinda sent a huge package of organic snacks as a gift. Before Jen asked for anything, she'd have to catch Melinda up on her condition.

She picked up her phone, called Melinda's private line. Melinda was delighted to get the call and learn Jen would be walking in a couple of weeks.

"I'll be on a cane," Jen said, "and I'll need lots of physical therapy, but I'll be mobile."

"Great. And what will you be doing work-wise?"

She explained about the loss of the Rotary job and the need to find something else. "Actually, I'm wondering if you would write me a reference letter."

"Be happy to. Now let me tell you about our activity in Africa." Melinda described the new round of the Village Advantage projects operating in almost thirty villages. "Ruth has worked out well, with Thabiri, of course. A good choice to take over from you."

"I'm glad, but jealous. Wish I were there."

Nathan poked his head in, and she waved at him to sit down.

"Jen," Melinda said, "while we were talking, an idea came to me. It won't get you to Africa but...Jen, I need someone to write up all the Foundation's activities in Africa for a major report to our Board and the public. I wonder if you'd be interested in doing some writing for us."

"How long a report do you want?"

"Quite long. Could be several hundred pages. You'd have to get up to speed on every disease and health strategy we work on. It's at least a six-month job."

"Really? That would be perfect, although I need a lot of rehab. I'd have to be in DC most of the time."

"You can work anywhere you like. So, you'll do it? I'd be so relieved."

"Of course, I'll do it." She gave Nathan a thumb's-up. "I can start tomorrow."

"Well, let's sign a contract first, but we'll start sending material tomorrow, some of it hard copy, some online."

"Melinda, thank you so much. You made my day."

She laughed. "I hope you're still saying that when you're buried in statistics on malaria. Bye, Jen. For now."

Jen put down her phone and reached for Nathan. He moved closer and she threw her arms around his neck. "You got me a job."

"Don't ever say something like that. You got the job. All your talent and hard work got you the job. I only suggested the phone call."

"Well, thanks for your brilliant suggestion." She gazed into his eyes. "How can we celebrate?"

"I can pop out for some champagne."

"Wait. Maddie left a bottle of prosecco in the fridge."

"Let me look." He shouted from the kitchen. "Bubbly in the garden?"

"With smoked oysters. There's a can in the cabinet next to the tuna."

She pushed out of bed, straightened her tee shirt and shorts, ran a brush through her hair. She grabbed her cane and shuffled toward the French doors. "I still need help to get outside," she called.

"Thank goodness you need me for something."

"Ha! I'll never be free of you."

"We'll see about that."

He opened the doors, put the prosecco on the garden table and helped Jen negotiate the step down. She asked him to bring her phone so she could text Maddie about her new job.

Dinner was delicious, especially washed down with prosecco.

"Nathan, when you showed up tonight, I was at an all-time low. I was sulking, which is rare for me. Now I'm at 85 or 90 percent. What a difference!"

He took her hand. "What would get you to 100 percent?"

"Oh, gee, going somewhere, I guess." She gave him a crooked smile. "Not anyplace far, maybe someplace a few minutes away."

He looked puzzled.

"I want to go upstairs and take a bath," she cried. "With oils and bubbles, water up to my chin. Do you know how long it's been since I had a bath?"

"A couple of months?"

"A couple of long, torturous months."

He got up, ambled over to the outer garden door, leaned against it for a few moments, deep in thought then came back. "I think we could do it."

Her forehead wrinkled. "Do what?"

"Get you upstairs. If you lean on me instead of your hip, and we go slowly, really slowly, well, it's only eleven steps. You want to try?"

"Nathan, you're serious." She pushed up from her chair. "Of course, I want to try."

He helped her up the step from the garden to the living room and followed her to the stairs. He placed her next to the railing, stood beside her, lowered himself and put her arm around his neck. "Comfortable?"

"Yes."

"Now, take a step with your right foot then I'll lift you up on the left side. Just don't put any weight on your left hip."

She giggled. "Like Siamese twins."

"Kind of. Shall we try?"

After a couple of steps, they got into a rhythm of "right leg, step, left leg, raise." After each step, Nathan said, "Atta girl."

When they reached the top, Jen leaned in and kissed him on the neck. "I can't believe we did that."

"Wait. Don't move without your cane."

He ran back downstairs. Back upstairs, he had handed it to her.

"In my closet, there's an aqua robe, a caftan. Could you get it for me?"

He brought it, saying, "Enjoy your soak. I'm going to do the dishes. Call me when you're done."

"Not so fast. I need help getting into the tub."

He heaved a sigh. "Didn't think of that."

She laughed. "You need to carry me over the side. I'll stand and when the water is up, you can hold me from the back and I'll slide down. And don't say anything about my scars."

"You're okay with this?"

"One hundred percent."

Chapter 30

Jen gloried in a long soak in a bath filled with bubbles, lavender salts and oils. When the water had cooled, she called to Nathan for help in getting out of the tub. He dashed upstairs and tried to assess the situation without staring at Jen's naked body.

"Don't worry about niceties," she quipped. "You've seen women's bodies before. You need to slide me out either from the back or over the side."

"There's more room at the back. How about if I stand behind you, put my arms through yours and lift?"

"That's what I thought."

They got into position and he lifted her easily. "You weigh next to nothing."

"I've lost weight. Hospital cuisine." She grabbed the towel. "Can you hand me the caftan?"

She slipped on the caftan. "I want just one more thing before we make our way down the mountain. I want to lie on my bed for a few minutes, and I'd love you beside me."

Using her cane, she limped down the short hall to her bedroom and lowered herself onto the bed. "Heaven, pure heaven. That hospital bed is so depressing." She patted the far side of the bed. "Nathan, try it."

He lay down and shut his eyes.

"Good, isn't it?"

"Not bad at all."

He reached over, took her hand. They lay quietly, staring at the ceiling. "It's not as beautiful as Zanzibar," he said, "but just as peaceful."

"Nathan, our lives are going to change in the next few weeks. I'll be working again. You'll be getting ready to teach. Soon I'll be able to put weight on my hip and move around."

"Bye-bye, hospital bed. I can get your couch back in a day."

She turned her head toward him. "I hope we'll still have dinners together."

"Of course, although maybe not every night."

She took a deep breath, exhaled then said, "You and I have an unusual relationship."

"I wouldn't say unusual. It's a strong friendship that developed in unusual circumstances."

"Agreed." She rolled over on her side to face him. "Have you ever thought of something more intimate? You know, the boy-girl kind of thing?"

"Of course, I've thought of it. Many times. But it wouldn't work."

"Why not?"

"Lots of reasons, none because of you, all because of me."

Jen flashed on Patricia's words. Something was blocking him. "Why do you say that?"

He let go of her hand. "Jen, I could never provide for you financially. Since my divorce, my resources are limited."

"Nathan, I would never expect you to provide for me. I've taken care of myself all my life and intend to keep doing so."

"There are always emerg—"

"Like my accident?"

"As one example."

"Well, health insurance is covering all the medical. The only thing I can't do without is you."

He took her hand again and squeezed it. "Thank you. Shall we go back downstairs?"

"If you can handle me."

They got up, moved to the top of the stairs and arranged themselves. Jen gripped the bannister next to the wall, her left arm hooked around Nathan's neck. They descended, step by step, with him carrying much of her body weight. She got back on the hospital bed and he brought her a mug of tea.

"Have you got a bit more time?" she asked.

"Sure."

"Good, 'cause I'd like to know your other reasons."

"Oh, Jen." He ran his fingers through his hair. "I'm not Mark. He's handsome, fit, tan, looks like a tennis player."

"Squash."

He smiled. "Squash player."

"And you want me to have a boy-toy?"

"Don't you?"

"Hardly. My attraction to Mark was never his looks. I appreciate his smarts and, I guess you could say, charm. But you have all of that and more."

"That's kind, but I'm not in the same class as Mark,"

"Jesus." She plunked her mug down on the nightstand. "You're not rich enough, handsome enough…what else?"

"Young enough." He grimaced. "You can't counter that one."

"Nathan, I'm 43, you're 60. Seventeen years. Has our age difference affected our relationship in any way?"

"Not yet, but…"

"Are you worried about a physical relationship?"

He shrugged.

She laughed. "I hope sometime we find out. For now, let's try one thing."

She patted the bed beside her. He sat down and she pulled his head toward her and kissed him passionately on the lips. He responded readily, taking her head in both his hands.

When they drew apart, she said with a smile, "Well, that's a start."

Chapter 31

Dr. Patel stared intensely at the x-rays on his computer screen. "Ms. Jacobs, you did well. Your hip will be stiff for some time, but physical therapy will take care of that. Congratulations."

"So, I'm free? I can climb stairs, take a bath, sleep in my own bed?" Jen asked with excitement.

"When you walk, you should use a cane until the therapist says otherwise, but, yes, you're free. What are you going to do first?"

She checked her watch. Three p.m. "Get a haircut, shampoo, blow-dry. All the armor a woman needs to take on the world."

"Well, the world awaits. Good luck."

"Thanks, Dr. Patel. When I walk by the hospital, I'll wave at you and cheer I'm not inside." She shook his hand. "Happy Labor Day."

At the hair salon a few blocks away, Jen texted Maddie and Miriam to tell them the good news. After her hair appointment, she would meet Nathan at Lincoln Center for a free jazz performance at Millennium Stage. Then, for the sake of nostalgia, she was taking him to dinner at the Watergate sushi bar.

They ordered, sake, sashimi, and a selection of sushi rolls. Nathan toasted her freedom. "Good-bye, George Washington Hospital."

"Except for the therapist, but I hear he's a cute Chinese-American, so that part should be fun."

"Trying to make me jealous?"

"You bet. Now, your turn. Tell me about your adorable students."

Nathan had already met with his American University students a few times and was charged up about teaching. At the same time, he was shocked by their ignorance of the developing world. He felt obliged to re-do his syllabi and incorporate introductory readings before tackling more advanced debates in the development field.

"The only way these kids will ever get it," he said, "would be to spend a month in Africa visiting urban slums, drought-starved villages, or refugee camps to see for themselves."

"Seems I made that point to you once upon a time? Nathan, some of your students will never get it, but others will take more courses, travel to Africa and Asia, even choose careers at USAID. Take me as an example."

"What about you?"

"I knew very little about Africa until I started working in overseas study. When I first met you, I knew next to nothing."

"Jen, you came to me because you wanted overseas students in Africa to leave their urban campuses and experience field work."

"Right. And we didn't change the world by providing two weeks of field experience, but we made a start."

"And that brought us together." He took her hand.

"That and Zanzibar."

～

When they got back to Jen's house, she felt embarrassed by the disarray of the living room. The Gates Foundation had sent her nine cartons of material on their African projects, which was spread in piles across her living room floor. She was grateful Nathan had been able to keep her couch so she had enough floor space to arrange the studies and reports by topic and region. In place of the couch, she had ordered a glass slab to hold her computer and files, a wood cabinet for the printer and supplies, and a card table for reference books and UN reports.

"Before I was deluged with all this," she told Nathan, "I'd been planning to cook you some nice meals, but there's no place to sit. Sorry for the mess."

"No worries. It's work. How about letting me cook a nice meal for you?"

"You've been cooking for me for over a month."

He grinned. "That was putting simple things together. I'm considering some fancy Italian recipes."

"Pasta to plump me up?"

"Lots of it. How about the day after tomorrow?"

"Great. Sometime after rush hour and the Metro crush?"

He placed his hands on her shoulders, pulled her close in a hug. "See you Thursday."

∽

Thursday evening, Jen took the Metro to Capitol Hill and walked the seven blocks to Nathan's low-rise, old-style apartment building. By the time she arrived, she was tired, and pain throbbed in her hip. She was grateful the building had an elevator to take her to the fourth floor.

Hearty odors of garlic and oregano seeped under the apartment door. Opera was playing loudly, and he didn't hear her knock. She had to phone to get him to answer the door.

"Sorry," he said, taking her jacket. "Verdi to go with the pasta."

She looked around the empty space – large rooms, long windows, traditional molding, attractive despite the lack of furniture. "This will be lovely once you fix it up."

"I'm saving all my paychecks. Thank goodness for your couch."

"Are you making spaghetti and meatballs?"

"Ravioli with spicy sausage from Eastern Market."

"Even better." She collapsed on the couch, patted the seat. "I'm gifting this baby to you. It suits the room and it's too big for my place."

"Jen, someday all those papers will be gone. You'll want the couch back."

"Nope. I'm getting two armchairs instead. Thanks to Bill and Melinda, I can splurge."

He brought her a glass of red wine and a dish of Eastern Market olives. She realized she was relishing their domesticity. A partner and a home life – something she hadn't known she was missing until she had it. Now she had just what she wanted -- the right amount of togetherness, them alone, no kids, nannies, family demands, just them.

They chatted about his classes and her plunge into African diseases, Bill Gates' passion. "Nate, I'm relieved to say I'm almost through the familiarization stage. In a few days, I begin drafting."

"Moving along."

"I need to finish the first draft by the Uganda conference in early December. Then all I'll have to do is polish it in January."

"Uganda?"

"Yup. It's a long trip, but they're flying me first class."

He laughed. "You picked the right employer. It's gonna spoil you for the rest of the nonprofit world."

He headed for the kitchen while she poured more wine. "Ready to eat?" he called out.

"More than ready."

Nathan's portion size was large, but she cleaned her plate. "Fantastic sausage. The next time you buy some, please get some for me." She reached into her shirt pocket and pulled out a folded piece of paper. "I've got a guessing game for dessert. Ready?"

"Is it about Africa?"

"No way. Here's your question. What do you, George Clooney, Warren Beatty, Harrison Ford, and Leonardo di Caprio have in common?"

"Easy. We're all handsome, rich and famous."

"Close, but no cigar. Keep guessing."

"You're not serious."

"Completely serious. You all have something in common."

"We're all actors? Directors?"

She shook her head. "I'll help. DiCaprio – 23, Harrison – 22, Beatty – 21, Clooney – 17."

"That's no help at all."

She looked down at her paper. "Okay. Another clue. Michael Douglas – 25, Alec Baldwin – 26, Sean Penn – 32, Richard Gere – 34."

"Listen, I like the company, but I don't belong in it."

"Yes, you do. Think."

He crossed his arms over his chest, frowned. After a couple of minutes, he said, "Game over. Nothing comes. Tell me."

"Every one of those men has a significant age difference with his partner or wife, from George Clooney at 17 years up to Richard Gere at 34. Gosh, that list puts us at the minimum."

He chortled. "You did your research. I have to hand you that."

Jen stood up. "Think about it. I've been thinking about it, and I just don't see our age difference as an obstacle to our being together."

He also stood. "Can I drive you home?"

"Thanks, but I'm going to take Uber." She kissed his cheek. "I'm going up to see Maddie and Patricia this weekend and take a break from my cluttered living room. Dinner on Monday?"

"Let's eat here. That'll give me all weekend to prepare."

"It's a deal."

Chapter 32

A week earlier, when Jen had texted Mark about her return home, he had texted back he was in Tahoe for the Labor Day weekend with the kids and Suzanne.

She couldn't resist. "Suzanne?"

He had texted back, "Kate's teacher. She loves kids but can't have any. Even loves the twins."

Now, when Jen got home from Nathan's, she found an email from Mark to give him a call. She did so immediately. They talked for a while about Jen's report for the Gates Foundation and Mark's Fall seminar on European influences on American thought.

While they had always kept their personal lives private, at a certain point in the conversation Jen's curiosity about Suzanne took over. "You mentioned Suzanne in your last text. How lovely that Kate has a teacher who's also a family friend."

"More than a friend. We've become a couple, at least on weekends. She's a kind of a surrogate mother for the kids."

"That's terrific. I've been hoping you'd find someone like her."

"She was right under my nose. We went for coffee after a PTA meeting and that was it. What about you?"

Jen didn't feel ready to open up about Nathan and the huge role he played in her life. Instead, she said, "Right now, I've got no room for anything except malaria, HIV and Ebola. Someday, I hope."

After her call with Mark, Jen made her way upstairs to pack her bag for the weekend. Going to Storrs and Maddie felt like going home – familiar house, familiar scenery, the warmth of a close friend, and an escape from tropical diseases.

∼

It turned out Maddie had big personal news as well. Patricia was moving in soon and would become a commuter to her work in Hartford. Jen was thrilled. Despite her taste for fun and adventure, Maddie had often seemed to be searching for companionship, and Patricia was a fine match.

The three women went out to a country inn on Saturday night to celebrate their partnership. The dining room was all oak beams, white table cloths, and carnations on the table. Couldn't be more traditional, not Maddie's usual style, but she raved about the roast beef and Yorkshire pudding.

Over a full-bodied shiraz, Jen shared the news about Mark and Suzanne. "He, too, has found the perfect partner. She adores kids, adores *his* kids. That's probably the most important thing to Mark in any relationship."

Maddie held up her wine glass, gazed at the deep burgundy color. "You know what that means, don't you?"

"No, what?"

"You're the only one without a partner. You need to do something about that. Quick."

Jen recounted the exchange she'd had with Nathan about why, in his view, he wasn't right for her. She shared the guessing game she'd played over age differences. They'd laughed then Patricia held up her hand. "May the counselor have the floor?"

"Of course," Jen said, "I need all the help I can get."

"Well, your game was cute, but think about it. You're asking Nathan to compare himself with di Caprio or Harrison Ford. That doesn't exactly build confidence."

"Damn. You're right. So, what do I do now?"

"Well, you know him best. What could convince him to be there for you?"

Jen cocked her head. "He is there, just not romantically."

"Let me put it differently. What makes Nathan unique?"

Closing her eyes to think, she knew immediately. "This will sound unromantic but it's his extraordinary willingness and readiness to help."

"Not at all unromantic," Maddie said. "He rushes home from Africa to be with you after your accident. He comes to the hospital every day then stays with you at home to help. That isn't duty; that's love."

Patricia jumped in. "The point is, he needs you. Yes, you need him, but he also needs you. He's got to know you need more than commitment, you also need passion."

Maddie grabbed Patricia's hand. "You got it, girlfriend. If Nathan thinks he can help Jen by romancing her, he'll be there faster than his trip home from Africa."

"How do I do this? Send him an email saying I need romance? Hang a message from a sky plane?"

"Honey, we can't tell you how. You know him best. Just make sure he knows you *need* him in bed. It'll work."

Jen looked at her two friends, raised her glass and said, "I'm game."

"And let us know."

∾

On her flight back to D.C. from Hartford, Jen asked herself what she could bring Nathan as a house gift. He had dishes, kitchenware, a table and chairs, futon and a couch. That was about it. She could choose a poster for the walls, but art was such an individual thing.

She considered pillows for the couch but wanted something special.

Suddenly, it came to her. The fair trade store at Dupont Circle had exquisite products from all over the developing world.

∽

The next morning, after several trying hours studying tables on maternal mortality, Jen took off for a shopping expedition. Within a half hour, she was browsing through the fair trade shop. Pillow covers from Rwanda jumped out at her. A surprisingly subdued African print in aqua, amber and tan with a giraffe embroidered on one pillow, an elephant on the other. She loved them and knew Nathan would, too.

∽

That evening, as she walked from the Metro to Nathan's, she found herself feeling anxious. She'd promised Maddie and Patricia she'd find a way to "romance" Nathan, but she couldn't throw herself at him. As it was, her game about age differences had probably gone too far. This was someone she cared about deeply. Showing him she needed romance had to be direct but also gentle.

"I've brought you something for the house," she announced as she came in the door.

"For the house?" he said, laughing. "Since I have next to nothing, I'm sure it will be sorely needed."

She reached into her shoulder bag for the package. "There's a second part of the gift, but I didn't have time to get them yet."

He opened the gift paper and pulled out the pillow covers. "How wonderful. Tanzania?"

"Next door. Rwanda."

He turned them over. "How do I hang them?"

"You don't. They're pillow covers. For the couch. I'll bring you the pillows the next time I'm here."

"Every time I sit on the couch, I'll think of you. Guess I do already."

He took her hand, pulled her toward the bedroom. "I also have a present for you."

He pushed open the door and gestured toward a king-size bed with light blue sheets and pillows and a white and blue striped comforter.

"For me?"

"For you. I didn't think you'd like sleeping on a futon."

"Wow. You even have sheets. I don't need to add a thing."

"Try it."

She sat down on the end of the bed then crawled to the middle and spread out her arms and legs. She flashed on Maddie and Patricia. "Nate, I love it, but I'm lonely. I need you here beside me."

He kicked off his moccasins and climbed next to her. She wrapped her arms around his neck and murmured, "I've wanted this for so long."

He pulled her close, kissed her mouth and neck then ran his hand under her jersey to her skin. She shivered with pleasure, began unbuttoning his shirt. He pulled off his shirt then his pants. "I don't want to hurt you."

"I'm fine on my side." She slid out of her slacks, pulled off her underwear. "Sorry for the scars."

"I love your scars. They're what brought us together."

They began to touch everywhere, continued for a long time. Then Jen thrust her leg over his and pulled him to her until they could wait no longer and he came inside. He rocked slowly then faster as Jen cried, "Nathan, I need you."

"I need you," he moaned as they rocked together until the end.

Eventually, Nathan pushed up onto one arm and took her breast in his other hand. Kissing it, said, "Dinner's going to be an anti-climax."

"Literally."

They burst into laughter and embraced again before putting on their clothes.

Nathan had splurged for dinner. Veal piccata, asparagus hollandaise, endive salad. Jen felt ecstatic, about more than the cuisine.

"I'm going to have to go away more often," she proclaimed as they finished eating. "By the way, Maddie and Patricia send their love."

He grinned. "Now that you can sleep here, they can have your place when they visit."

"Only when I finish that blasted report. I've got to buckle down. I'm behind schedule."

"A self-imposed schedule."

"True, but it's still got to get done by Uganda."

Chapter 33

The next few months were rewarding for Jen and Nathan. Their weekdays were devoted to work with an occasional evening together for a bite to eat. Nathan was consumed by teaching, Jen, by writing. She tried to make her report as lively as possible by injecting sketches about individual Africans into her data summaries. She gleaned the stories from Gates Foundation staff eager to contribute anecdotes about some of their favorite participants. Melinda was delighted by Jen's approach.

Jen and Nathan spent the weekends taking idyllic breaks, often enjoying an overnight excursion to the Maryland shore or Virginia countryside. They evolved into a real couple, sharing domesticity as well as fun, planning their schedules together, and dreaming about projects like team-teaching at American University or taking work-travel trips to the developing world.

One brisk Fall afternoon as they walked along the Potomac, Nathan floated an idea he'd been secretly researching. "You know, it seems kind of a shame for you to go all the way to Uganda and not take some time off for a safari."

"They aren't paying me to safari."

"Okay, but they're not expecting your final report before mid-January. You'd have plenty of time to wrap it up even after a few additional days in Africa."

"You're leading up to something."

"Well, I did have a thought I might come meet you and do a little more of that trip that got cut short."

She grimaced. "By me."

"It was my call. You were unconscious."

She took his hand. "What did you, do you, have in mind?"

"I thought I might meet you in Windhoek."

"Windhoek? Namibia's more than 2000 miles from Uganda."

"It's a long flight. Actually, several flights due to stops. Ten hours."

"You checked. And you know I've always wanted to go there."

"So you said when we set up the field experience for overseas students."

Jen was stunned he'd remembered from years before. "What kind of Namibia experience are you thinking of?"

"National parks, sand dunes, the Atlantic Coast. With our own Jeep and driver."

"What?" She stopped in her tracks. "Such luxury?"

"Well, a happy coincidence. One of my buddies, Charlie Evans, from my time as Africa Director at AID, is now the Namibia Mission Director. He invited me and offered his Jeep and driver to tour the country. All we'd have to pay is gas, accommodations, and the driver's tip."

"Incredible. Charlie sounds like more than a buddy."

"I did him a few favors."

Jen dropped her cane, put her hands on his shoulders. "Can we really do this?"

"We can make an itinerary when we get home."

"Oh, Nathan. What a gift. I doubt Melinda will have a problem."

He picked up her cane and gave it to her, took her other arm to continue their walk. After a few minutes, Jen conceded she was getting tired. They turned around and walked back to Nathan's car.

Once back at his place, he poured two wines, and they settled on the couch.

"Just one minute." He disappeared into the bedroom and returned, smiling.

"Why the smile?"

"Well, I just remembered one problem related to our trip. The Namibian government is rather conservative. They don't allow coed singles to sleep together in hotels. Only married couples can rent rooms together."

Jen and Nathan had previously agreed neither was interested in marriage. Their partnership covered all their needs.

"So, we fake it," Jen said. "I've got no problem with that."

"Me neither, but this might help our case." He reached into his pocket and pulled out a gray velvet jewelry box.

"Nate…"

"Just open it. I can always take it back."

"Nathan, I—"

"Just open it."

Inside was an emerald-cut stone of the most extraordinary blue color set in a modest diamond band.

"It's not fake, just a bit different. The color changes in different lights."

She fixed her gaze on him. "I have to ask. What is it?"

"First, try it on."

She slipped the ring on her ring finger. The color first gave off an intense sapphire blue then, when she tilted her wrist, a deep violet. "I can't believe it. It's amazing."

"It has a special meaning for us. It's Tanzanite. You can guess where it comes from."

"Perfect, but I can't accept it." She tried to slip it off but he clutched her hand. "Jen, it's a partnership ring. I'm not proposing. We have a partnership. I'm ready to let others know. If you like it, wear it for us."

She gently kissed his lips. "I'll wear it and treasure it."

He laughed. "That will make the Namibian hotel industry very happy."

~ 2012 ~

"Sorry it took so long to get back to you," Mark said.

"No problem. I knew you'd connect eventually. What's new?" Jen asked.

"Another book coming out in the Fall."

"Whew. You are prolific. What's this one about?"

"Oriental thinking, a comparison of Eastern and Western mindsets. I worked with a Chinese historian visiting Stanford. It's also coming out in Chinese."

"Pretty heavy. Sounds like I'll need a month to read it."

"It'll be worth it."

So Mark. "Modest as always."

"How about you?" he said.

She sighed. "You won't believe this, but I'm thinking of retiring. Well, not actually retiring but turning my firm over to a colleague."

"How will you stay busy?"

"Nathan and I will team-teach one semester."

"At American University?"

"American in Nairobi, maybe Tel Aviv sometime in the future."

He chuckled. "Back to overseas studies. Isn't that how you two met?"

"Yup. A long time ago."

There was a pause in the conversation. They were always glad to chat but seemed to have less and less to say, perhaps because they generally kept their personal lives out of bounds. Except for Mark's kids.

"Did I tell you Kate got into Yale?"

"I'm not surprised. New Haven will be a change from Palo Alto."

"She says she wants a change." He cleared his throat. "We'll see how long that lasts."

"And the twins?"

"They're kind of going their own ways, which we've encouraged. Michael's into basketball; Peter is all caught up in art."

"No competition there."

"Oh, they still compete. They're twins."

Jen could see him rolling his eyes.

"Hey, one big piece of news," he said. "I'm going on sabbatical. First time in fifteen years. Suzanne won over."

"Fantastic. What are your plans?"

"Only one trip. Maybe a family safari."

"After your first one got canceled?" she asked.

"Something like that. Who knows? We might cross paths in Nairobi."

Jen knew that would never happen. Meeting as couples, going through polite formalities, that would change the friendship. And they didn't want to do that. Through everything – the times when they'd been closer, now connecting with only occasional calls – the friendship had held.

"I can wear my tee shirt."

"Did you ever figure out 'fnfe'?"

"Partly. Friends now, friends…"

"Yes, we're friends. But fnfe is *for now, forever.*" He laughed. "We made that work."

"We certainly did."